The Deptford Mouselets
Fleabee's Fortune

ROBIN JARVIS

Hodder
Children's
Books

a division of Hodder Headline Limited

Fleabee's Fortune

Books for older readers
by Robin Jarvis:

THE DEPTFORD MICE

The Dark Portal
The Crystal Prison
The Final Reckoning

THE DEPTFORD HISTORIES

The Alchymist's Cat
The Oaken Throne
Thomas

THE WHITBY WITCHES

The Whitby Witches
A Warlock in Whitby
The Whitby Child

Visit the author's website:
www.robinjarvis.com

Chapters

Characters

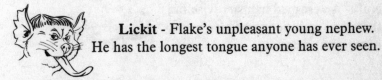

Fleabee - A young ratgirl who is unlike the rest of her kind. She cannot bring herself to harm anything and spends her days dreaming.

Scabmona - Fleabee's younger sister. She is a true rat of Deptford and a real terror. She cannot wait to peel her first mouse.

Klakkweena - Mother of Fleabee and Scabmona. She is a typical ugly ratwife who likes nothing better than to start an argument.

Rancid Alf - Father of Fleabee and Scabmona. He is a lazy good-for-nothing, and is a perfect match for Klakkweena.

Lickit - Flake's unpleasant young nephew. He has the longest tongue anyone has ever seen.

Flake - A crony of Rancid Alf. He has a remarkable skin complaint and is always scratching.

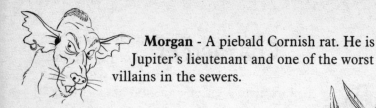

Morgan - A piebald Cornish rat. He is Jupiter's lieutenant and one of the worst villains in the sewers.

Wormy Ned - One of the few rats who can read. He keeps the book of Ratiquette in which all Jupiter's laws are written down.

Vinegar Pete - A sour-faced grumbler who never smiles.

Leering Macky - A rat with a dreadful squint. He and Vinegar Pete are always muttering to one another.

Ambrose - A young grey squirrel from Greenwich. Grey squirrels are jittery and nervous, and Ambrose is no exception.

Nuff - An escaped hamster with big theatrical ambitions and an eye for flamboyant detail.

Tilik and Vasili - Gerbil brothers from Mongolia who escaped from captivity with Nuff. They speak very little English but are excellent acrobats.

'Orace Baldmony - The first rat ever to have rebelled against the will of Jupiter and who went to live a less violent life with mice. Unfortunately his new life did not last long.

Madame Akkikuyu - A fraudulent fortune-telling black rat from Morocco. She specialises in peddling fake charms and potions.

The Raith Sidhe
(pronounced Rayth Shee)-
The Three ancient Gods of the rats who ruled long before Jupiter crept into the sewers. For over a thousand years they have been sleeping, but now they are seeking a way back into the living world.

Jupiter - The mysterious and fearsome God of the rats. He dwells in the dark portal and possesses awesome powers.

1

A flower in the Dark

The final breaths of night were still whiffling through the city of London. A dismal rain had passed over and darkness filled the glistening streets, but already the deep shadows were shrinking before the approaching dawn.

Soon the sodden sparrows would stir. Atop dripping buildings and monuments, in muddy parks and graveyards they would begin to sing and welcome the waking day, and the world would stretch and blink and yawn.

Yet far beneath the drowned roads and crowded estates, another country rested – secure and secret in a deeper darkness. Below the borough of Deptford, down the gurgling drains and in the dank dark of the sewers, eternal night presided.

Through those old arched channels, rivers of filthy water slopped and swilled, flowing endlessly in the blind blackness – splashing the ancient brickwork with slime and stinking ooze. The noise of the moving waters echoed ceaselessly from chamber to chamber, but there were other sounds, other voices to be heard in that foul gloom.

Along a narrow ledge, high above the chasing floods a small furry figure picked her way, humming croakily to herself.

At a sharp corner, where three tunnels converged in a great high space she paused and raised her face to the invisible heights above.

'Mouldy maggots and crawling bacon!' she shouted at the top of her small voice. From the murk a hundred versions of her cry came bouncing back and she chuckled to herself.

With an ungainly wobble she sat down, dangled her feet over the ledge and waited.

Gradually the swallowing darkness began to lift. In one of the vaulting curves of the ceiling a frown-shaped duct led straight to the upper world and through this narrow way the dawn came slanting.

Brick by brick the chamber crept out of the night. Pale rays moved across the rushing waters and were instantly broken and scattered – cast into the furthest shadowy holes.

Upon her perch, the small figure held her breath: she marvelled at the new blossoming colours, the rich reds of the bricks and the yellow foam that crested the bronze rapids below. And then the swelling light reached her.

Her grubby toes wriggled as the first beams met them and she gave a throaty squeal of pleasure. Over her happy form the morning moved, over her shaggy brown fur, on to her tightly clasped claws, curving around the stone beads that adorned her neck, sparkling in the dew on her pink nose and blazing in the soft brown of her gentle eyes.

Her long tail twitched and flicked behind her and the ratgirl hugged herself a little tighter. She loved this place.

Fleabee had lived in the sewers for the whole of her ratling life. The outside world was just a vague and remote region she had only heard about in dubious stories told by her father and his scurvy cronies. Her young mind could not begin to understand what they meant when they spoke of ridiculous-sounding things like 'sky' or 'stars' or 'waste ground'. It was an essential

13

part of Ratiquette to tell as many lies as possible and she assumed that these peculiar, nonsensical notions were yet more clumsy scraps of tall-tale embroidery.

For Fleabee, the dripping sewer roof was the only sky she had ever known; the only green and growing things she had encountered were sickly mosses that sprouted between the brickwork and leaves flushed down the grids and gutters. No shape of tree or cloud ever brightened the landscape of her thoughts, but she compensated in many ways.

Lately she had taken to roaming the tunnels a little bit further each day and finding new places where the mysterious light found its way in from outside. So far this was her favourite early morning spot, where the dawn light revealed a wondrous cathedral-like cavern of brick arches, but there were many other sites she was equally fond of.

Midday often took her to a very wide sewer where she would sit on a rusted chain and watch shafts of dazzling light push through holes in the metal circles set high above. As vertical rods those beams lit her world and she never tired of gazing at them and the shifting kaleidoscope they made upon the water. Other times of day took her to tunnels where the bricks glittered gold and on brilliant nights, ghostly silver. Fleabee was certain that no other rat had bothered to even notice these things. They were her own private magicks and that made her love them even more.

Presently the dawn light began to dim. The sun was rising in the world outside and the ratgirl's cavern was sinking into darkness once more. The smile on her pleasant plump face dwindled too and she knew it was time to return home.

Wiping her nose across her arm, she rose to her feet and plodded back along the narrow ledge.

As she approached the main tunnels at the heart of the rat domain, Fleabee's heart hung heavy in her chest. Countless holes and gaps riddled the walls around her and flaming torches flared and smoked, scorching and blackening the bricks. This was where the rats of Deptford dwelt. They were a bloodthirsty army of cut-throats and villains, and her family was no exception.

The familiar shrieking arguments resounded in many noxious dens as she continued on her way. If a rat has something to say, it's worth yelling and growling about was a lesson that had been shouted into her from the earliest age.

Several sharp-faced sneering snouts leaned out of their holes as she passed by. Some spat, others snorted – across the tunnel one of them threw back his head and laughed harshly.

'Here she comes!' jeered a particularly ugly ratwife who was slumped against a scruffy-looking entrance.

'What a show-up that girl is. Why don't you mess your hair or rub some slime in it? Ain't you shamed to be so groomed? A right good thumping is what you need! Should be chucked into the black muds, you should!'

Fleabee halted and looked up at the slovenly creature. Strips of faded rags hung from her shoulders, a single fang jutted from her bottom lip and her head was crowned with a wigwam of bristles, made from a discarded brush, that covered her own lank, greasy hair.

'Good morning, Mother,' said Fleabee.

Another raucous laugh burst from across the tunnel.

'Good?' shrieked the ratwife in outrage. 'Good? Don't you dare be polite – you little horror. Get in!'

A knobbly clenched foot kicked the ratgirl through the hole and she hopped into the squalid nest, followed by her angry parent.

'I'll learn you to make a joke of me!' the ratwife bawled. 'I'll mucky your mouth with dung if you say owt like that again. That's no way fer a rat to speak. Show some disrespect! My old dad would turn in his grave if he could hear you and if we'd been mad enough to bury him. What are we to do with you?'

Fleabee's mother, Klakkweena, was a daughter of the famous Black Ratchet – one of the most wicked and cruel rats ever to have lived. In his time Black Ratchet had been revered as the worst of them all, and his descendants still made use of his memory when it suited them.

'And what do you mean coming back here with not so much as a manky morsel dangling from your claws?' she screeched. 'What you been up to this time, you lazy fat baggage?'

Fleabee stared at the filthy uneven floor. 'Exploring,' she muttered.

'Exploring!' her mother wailed. 'We can't stuff our guts on exploring, can we? Too much like your no-good dad you are, always off with his layabout gang, gambling, idling and wasting the night. Here's me slaving away getting this hole as dirty and honking like an arm pit as I can and what for? You make me heave, you do!'

Fleabee had heard this rant many times before and knew there were several more shrieks to go before her mother would let her escape to her room.

'Who was it scraped and gouged this midden out of solid brick and stone with her bare claws and gnashers? You tell me that? Not your wormy father – oh no. Always leaves it to me – the louse-chewer. To

17

think I could've had my pick of that mangy crew but what did I do? I chose the most ...'

'Stinkful, vomit-faced weedy sot what ever slobbered!' finished a high voice as into the rat hole marched a girl half the size of Fleabee.

It was Scabmona, her young sister. She was everything a ratling of Deptford ought to be, and not a bit like Fleabee.

Scabmona was already the scourge of the neighbours and the sneaky pride of her parents. It was as if all the hate and wickedness had bypassed Fleabee and manifested in her.

She did her very worst to be as frightful and fearsome as she possibly could. Her squat form was always racing headlong into mischief, and her angry eyes were constantly darting in search of trouble and unwary victims to play her tricks or vent her temper upon. Her little body was usually afflicted with scabs, for she loved to cultivate them. She purposely grazed her knees and scuffed her elbows in order to enjoy a long pick and prod at the crusty wounds.

Her dumpy face was normally set for battle; she would fly into rages at the slightest remark and had recently taken to slicking her hair up into a spike on top of her head, to make herself feel taller and more threatening.

18

Klakkweena eyed her as the ratchild swaggered by. A grubby length of cotton trailed from the ratling's fist and tied to the end of it was a large cockroach. Scabmona had caught it over a week ago and had been the envy of the other youngsters. She kept it as a pet and took it for long walks up and down the tunnels.

'Come on, Growler,' she called, giving the thread a sharp tug. This flipped the insect on its back and it flailed the air with its many legs.

'Don't sneak off just yet,' her mother squawked. 'You seen your father? Where's the old misery got to this time? I'll wager he ain't out scroungin' summat sweet and rotten to feed our bellies ... Oi – you listening to me?'

Scabmona raised her palm and stomped off to the cramped sleeping quarters she shared with Fleabee. 'Talk to the claw 'cos the snout ain't listening!' she snorted.

Something like a smile twitched on to Klakkweena's face. 'Why can't you be more like her?' she hissed at Fleabee. 'She'll have nowt to worry about when it's time for her Firstblood. She'll be clobbering

19

someone good and proper well before then.'

Fleabee groaned and bit her lip, wondering for the umpteenth time why she felt so different from everyone else. She knew she was not like the others but did not understand why. She hated the grisly stories her father told and would often wince and close her eyes, whereas her sister would jump up and down demanding juicier and more gruesome details. Fleabee really was an oddity amongst that infernal mob.

No other living creature dared venture down to the rats' nightmarish realm. For many hundreds of years a terrible power had dwelt in the darkness of the sewers, watching and waiting, growing ever more powerful, relentlessly instilling his subjects with a savage bloodlust, and now the rats of Deptford were renowned as ferocious, murdering fiends.

Yet even they lived in terror of their living God, He who crouched in the shadows and plagued their dreams. The most brutal of them would whisper His name with awe and tug at their ears with fright. For this was the evil realm of Jupiter – Lord of All.

'Yes,' her mother drawled with folded arms and a sour expression across her snout. 'You're big enough to go out there and start thieving for yerself. I'd been filching and pouncing on the weak well before your age but just look at you! What sort of rat do you think you are? Won't be long now till the night of Firstblood and you know what happens to them what ain't never jabbed nor blue-murdered! And you'll only have yerself to blame!'

Fleabee nodded. The terrible rat festival of Firstblood was fast approaching. It was a horrific, violent time that every other rat looked forward to and revelled in. She had always found some excuse not to take part in previous years, but now it was expected of her and she was very afraid. The feast of Firstblood was not merely a night of wild carousing and peevish skirmishes – its purpose was very real and deadly.

Every ratling who had not yet despatched another creature was given one last chance to do so. But if they failed before midnight, then it was they who would be turned upon and killed.

With her tail dragging across the floor, Fleabee trudged off to her room, where Scabmona was already sniggering at her.

'Can't wait to get this place all to myself,' the awful child declared.

2

With Rancid Alf and his Cronies

F leabee spent the rest of the morning asleep in her
  nest, having pulled an old piece of sacking over
her head to blot out her sister's spiteful taunts.

Eventually even Scabmona tired of insulting her
and played for a while with Growler. But her fascination
with the cockroach was waning. It really was too tame
for such a savage owner and it wasn't long before her
head began to nod and she snored gruffly.

It was well past midday when their mother's
screeching voice jolted them both awake.

'What time do you call this?' she screamed.
'Dragging yer sorry carcass here without so much as a
snarl and what's that you got plastered all round yer
chops? Is that rotted apples? You been and found some

over-ripe pickin's and not brought any back fer me? Oh that's so like you that is, you stingy glutton – never a squirmy thought about us stuck here with nowt in our guts but rumbly wind and belly aches.'

Scabmona's eyes flashed. Evidently their father had returned. She bounded from her messy nest to go and enjoy the argument, hoping to see a fight. Unattended and off the leash, Growler scurried up the wall.

Fleabee rolled over. Like every rat couple, their parents were engaged in a prolonged war with one another. Peace rarely broke out, so this screaming match was nothing out of the ordinary.

Her father, Rancid Alf, was no different from any of the other unpleasant villains who lived in the Deptford sewers. He was sly and treacherous and had a bad word to say about everybody, but he saved the most poisonous insults for Klakkweena.

'What a toasty welcome this is!' his nasal voice snapped, as he staggered into the rat hole. 'My old heart baulks to see you too, my tatty, gripe-faced sickener. Why don't you ever do anything really useful, and go and jump on a trap? Is that too much for me to hope for?'

'Oh that'd suit you, wouldn't it Alf!' she raged. 'That'd leave you free to bring your stupid pals round to drink and gamble, you'd bet your very skin away if I weren't here – you grit-brained nit! Well if anyone's going to flay your dismal hide, it'll be me and it might just happen today!'

'Today?' he yelled back. 'Your tongue's that sharp it happens all the time. I reckon I know what a peeled mouse feels like, except them lucky little beggars only get to be skinned the once! A scorpion in a fur coat, that's what you are, only they ain't half so revoltin'!'

'You bandy-legged blue bottle!'

'Puke magnet!'

'Scratch him!' Scabmona cried, dancing around them. 'Bite him! Chew his ears off!'

Her father was an oddly-shaped specimen. The upper part of his body was all bone and gristle, with ribs visible through his thinning fur and shoulder blades scraping under the skin like sharp shovels. But his stomach bulged alarmingly as though he had gulped down a whole onion without chewing it. The weight of his round belly made him stoop and his thin tail would often wrap itself around pipes and large stones to keep him from falling over.

'So where have you been?' Klakkweena demanded.

Rancid Alf licked his teeth and gave a repulsive grin. His face was naturally pinched and untrustworthy but his eyes were large and red-rimmed and often swollen by a blow from her fists.

'Only went and found a great pulpy apple a-floatin' in the ooze,' he boasted. 'Had to jump in to fetch it.'

'You should have fetched it here!'

'Hear me out, oh pus-filled ulcer of my life. Your Alf ain't so cracked as you reckon him. I put that there squishy treasure to a purpose, there'll be dividends I tell you.'

Klakkweena's eyebrows slid together. 'What sort of dividends?' she asked suspiciously. 'What dim plots you cooked up this time?'

'Guess who I done shared my apple with.'

'If it was that slug-faced trollop Boglina, I'll make jam out of you then go round there and rip out her whiskers.'

Rancid Alf chuckled. 'Nah, it were one of the lads I let have a guzzle.'

'What fer?'

'Cos he got a spree lined up for tonight, see? And now he's gonna let me join him.'

A greedy smirk stole over Klakkweena's snout and she glanced warily at the entrance to make sure no one else could overhear them. 'What sort of spree?' she whispered.

'A plunder raid!' he said, with a lick of his lips. 'Fresh and flapping and tender, so he says.'

'You gonna burst someone?' squealed Scabmona gleefully. 'You gonna poke and jab and bloomerder 'em? I wanna come – I wanna do it! I wanna bloomer them. Let me – let me!'

'Quiet!' her mother barked. 'You want the whole tunnel to hear you? How much booty do you think'd be left fer us if they all found out about it?'

Scabmona covered her mouth at once. 'I didn't say nowt,' she burbled between her claws. 'Just let me come with you.'

But a new idea occurred to Klakkweena and she jerked her head towards the ratgirls' sleeping chamber. 'Take Fleabee,' she told her husband.

'What … her?' choked Rancid Alf. 'That useless lump in there? Why for?'

'So she don't shame us at Firstblood. We'd never hear the end of it. Folk are already yakking about her and sayin' as how we've been too soft. That Hagnakker crone three holes down was grinning like a split tomato before. Had to slap her one, I did. I tell you Alf, if Fleabee don't do what's only natural and make summat stone-dead, then I won't answer fer it.'

To Scabmona's dismay, her father was forced to agree. 'Even the lads have been making cracks about our goody two claws,' he muttered.

'That's settled then,' decided Klakkweena. 'She goes with you tonight and you stand over her and make sure she does what's needed!'

'Not fair!' Scabmona grumbled, kicking the wall. 'I want to go bloomer summat as well.'

'Go torment your cockroach,' her mother said sternly.

That evening Fleabee found herself taken from the family hole by her father and led away from the main rat tunnels.

Having been told what was expected of her, she was horribly nervous. Reluctantly she followed Rancid Alf, but kept telling herself that it was better to get this over with as soon as possible. She was, after all, a rat of Jupiter and had to prove herself loyal and worthy.

'Keep up, stop dawdlin'!' her father snapped as they hurried down smaller passageways. 'Not far now.'

Rancid Alf's bulb-shaped form scurried on ahead. A knotted string was tied about his stomach and three sharp knives hung at his side. Fleabee wondered just where they were going and which of his nasty friends they were meeting.

At the junction of two tunnels, where the ledge widened to a broad platform, he halted. He whipped around and pulled her against the wall next to him.

'This is where we waits,' he whispered. 'We'll be met here, won't be long now.'

Fleabee peered into the darkness around her and shuddered at the thought of what lay ahead for her that night.

'It's not mouseys is it, Dad?' she asked in a small voice. 'We're not going to ambush some mouseys and peel them, are we?'

'Mouseys?' cried a new voice from the thick black shadows a little distance away. 'Oh, wouldn't that be sweet now? Haven't had a good peeled mousey for ages. Oh I dreams of them, I does. Never a tastier, more succulent bite than a fresh mousey.'

As the stranger approached the platform where they stood, Fleabee pressed closer to her father. She was unnerved to see that the rat was not alone – three other figures were prowling behind him.

'Oi, Flake!' snarled her father. 'Who's them you've dragged along? I thought it was just gonna be you an' me on this 'ere raid.'

'Just you?' retorted the newcomer. 'Then who's that you've got tucked by you?'

'Only our Fleabee. Didn't think you'd mind. She'll not get in the way.'

The rat strode forward and sneered at her. Fleabee stared back at him. She had seen Flake many times in the company of her father. He was one of the ugliest rats in the sewers and had been named Flake because of the countless impressive and itching skin ailments that afflicted him. He truly was a wonder, and could scratch off more diseased skin than anyone else. Needless to say, Scabmona admired him greatly.

'You brought your fumigated Fleabee?' Flake said with a laugh in his voice.

'It was a mighty big apple!' Rancid Alf reminded him, before jabbing a suspicious claw at the other three rats. 'And how did they buy their places tonight?'

Flake rubbed his threadbare chest and stood aside so Rancid Alf could get a better view. 'Don't gnaw yer tail off,' he said. 'It's only Vinegar Pete and Leering Macky.'

One of these rats bared his fangs in a vile grin as his eyes rolled in their sockets, pointing in different directions. The other creature's face was not made for grinning; it simply grew slightly less sour than normal.

'They had some runny stuff with chewy lumps in they let me have a go at,' Flake explained. 'Don't you worry none. Where us are going there'll be plenty enough this night. 'Sides, this is a four-rat job.'

'So who's that little pudgy one at the back?' Alf demanded, still doubtful.

Flake smirked and beckoned to the short, round figure that had remained in the gloom.

Fleabee knew him at once. He was a ratling the same age as herself called Lickit. She had always tried to avoid him. He was a piggy piece of vermin who had the longest tongue anyone had ever seen. It dangled from his mouth like a ribbon of boiled ham and was always slobbering over something. He never said much but when he did, it was in a lisping, spit-fuelled sort of way.

'This 'ere's my nephew,' Flake told Rancid Alf. 'Since his dad upped and croaked, I does what I can fer the drooling wretch. Good job I brung him, he can keep your soppy girl company.'

At that, Lickit grabbed Fleabee's claw and before she could stop him, the ratboy dragged his tongue across it.

'That's how he says hello,' Flake laughed. 'Forever tastin' summat or other he is, it's more than a habit – a right drippy obsession.'

Fleabee shuddered and turned away, wiping the spit from her claw.

'Cut the yapping,' scowled Vinegar Pete. 'Let's get to it. I wants me dinner.'

Flake nodded vigorously and a drizzle of dead skin fell from his scalp. Some of it landed on Lickit's outstretched tongue and the ratling rolled it into his mouth, chuckling to himself.

'Dinner?' Flake cried. 'There's more than one dinner in this fer us. Keep our guts stuffed 'n' tight fer days, this night's work will. There's some real sweet pickin's just awaiting fer us to go snatch 'em.'

Slapping his tail on the bricks, he leaped down the tunnel and Rancid Alf, Leering Macky and Vinegar Pete went charging after him. Lickit pursued them, his repulsive tongue streaming about his ears like a pink banner.

Fleabee took a deep breath, then followed.

Through unfamiliar tunnels Flake took them, along seldom-used passageways, until at last they came to the crumbling end of a great rusted pipe.

'Now,' he addressed them, with a serious edge to his voice. 'You all know where this'll lead?'

Rancid Alf, Vinegar Pete and Leering Macky nodded

gravely; but for the benefit of Fleabee and his nephew, Flake added, 'This 'ere is a path to the big outside.'

He paused to let the revelation sink in. 'Us all knows that us can't leave these 'ere sewers without proper permission from the bosses, from Morgan or even Jupiter Hisself. Well, us ain't got no permission and the likes of me and you wouldn't never get none anyhow. It's forbid and they'd come down on our necks real hard if us were caught or someone snitched, so scrape the wax out yer lug-holes and listen to me. You split on me and by Jupiter, I'll split you, tail to snout, before Morgan's lackeys cart me off. This is strictly a private bit of filching. Us doesn't want no boastin' to no one about this an' I doesn't want no one coming back 'ere on their lonesome to try a bit of solo thievery. Does you understand that?'

Everyone nodded, even Lickit, who had sampled the rusty pipe with the tip of his tongue and was grimacing at the unpleasant metallic tang.

Flake's eyes gleamed in the darkness. 'From now on keep yer traps shut. Any talking needs doin', I'll do it.'

'Whatever you says,' Leering Macky whispered. 'We'll follow your lead in this, Flakey boy – it's your spree. You know what's what.'

'Don't you forget it! Now, let's go cram our bellies.'

Up the pipe he went and the other rats followed him – except Fleabee.

Her little heart was thumping in her chest. She had never been so close to the outside world before. The fresh clean airs of a March night were blowing down the pipe and ruffling her fur. Her nostrils thrilled at the wondrous, unimagined scents and the cramped tunnels of the sewers became a distant, unhappy memory of another life.

The ratgirl closed her eyes and let the soft breeze envelop her. For a moment she even forgot the dreadful task that lay ahead. Standing at the mouth of that rusted pipe, wrapped in the tantalising promise of the upper world, was the closest she had ever been to happiness.

'Shift yerself, you stupid dollop!' her father's voice hissed at her, and the moment was gone.

Rancid Alf hurried back to his daughter and gave her a shake. 'Don't you make a fool out of me tonight!' he growled. 'Don't you dare let me down in front of these lads or you won't even live to see Firstblood.'

Taking one of the knives from his string belt he pressed it into her claws. 'You'll need this,' he told her. 'And make sure you use it!'

Seizing Fleabee's arm he dragged her into the pipe and the ratgirl was compelled to trot alongside.

The other rats had already gone through the pipe. Now a glowing circle of dull orange light lay before Fleabee and her father.

She wondered what it could be. Was that the same light that poured into the sewers during the day to wake the hidden colours and make them dance? Soon she would know. Every step brought the end of the pipe closer and the excitement bubbled within her.

Then, with a leap, they were through. Rancid Alf pulled her clear and they were outside, in the upper world.

3

The Plunder Raid

Before she could even look about her, Fleabee felt
her feet splash into soft mud and so her first
glimpse of this strange country was of grey silt rising
up between her toes. She smiled. This mud was clean
to the touch, not like the foul-smelling sludge of
her home.

Then she lifted her gaze and almost cried out in fear
and joy.

She was standing on the banks of Deptford Creek, a
narrow waterway that flowed into the River Thames.
But to Fleabee the expanse was enormous. Her mind
had never conceived of such an open space. The water
sparkled with the reflected light of street lamps and it
was this electric glare that she had seen from within

the pipe. Gradually her eyes lifted from the twinkling creek and at last she beheld the sky.

Dark clouds smudged and smeared the heavens, but here and there a cold white star shone bravely. The instant she saw them, those tiny points impaled her bright young soul.

There were no words in her clumsy rat vocabulary to describe her first sight of the stars, but tears brimmed in her eyes and she held her breath.

Nothing she had ever heard had prepared her for this. A great sob welled up in her breast as tears streaked down her furry snout.

'Plaguey filth!' her father cursed in a whisper. 'Where've they got to?'

Ignorant of the emotion that had possessed his daughter, Rancid Alf cast about for the others.

The shore was littered with broken prams and half-submerged shopping trolleys. His bulging eyes peered into their shadows. A movement caught his attention and he whisked his head about swiftly.

There, standing behind the arch of a partly buried tyre, were Flake and the rest. Alf rubbed his claws together and nudged Fleabee in the ribs with his bony elbow.

'Here we go. This is where the fun starts!'

Taking care not to make a sound, he set off for the tyre and, with her face still lifted to the night sky,

Fleabee wiped away the tears and followed.

'Does you see it, lads?' Flake muttered when they joined them. 'Does you see that treasure just a-waiting to be snapped up?'

His scaly claw poked at the air and everyone stared along the bank. Remembering her father's stern words, Fleabee wrenched her eyes away from the stars. But at the water's edge, where Flake was pointing, she could see only a jumble of twigs and driftwood.

'What we goggling at?' Leering Macky asked, his mismatched eyes roving to and fro. 'Nowt there.'

'You havin' a laugh?' Vinegar Pete said bitterly.

'Patience,' Flake assured them. 'And keep quiet. See – look now!'

Within the dark mass of driftwood, something stirred. A mottled brown head upon a slender neck rose from the twigs and was silhouetted against the glimmering water.

Vinegar Pete drew a sharp breath and sucked on his fangs, while Leering Macky made a low rattling gurgle in his throat. Rancid Alf was trembling with expectation. Only Fleabee and Lickit were confounded.

'What ith it?' Lickit asked.

His uncle heaved a delighted sigh. 'A duck in its nest,' he murmured. 'An' why do ducks make nests?'

'To sleep in and keep warm?' suggested Fleabee.

The rats held on to the tyre and laughed as quietly as they could manage.

'To lay their eggs,' Rancid Alf told her. 'Oh – duck eggs is dee-lish. I haven't guzzled on a yolk in years.'

Flake wagged a claw at him. 'Too late fer that,' he hissed, nodding at the nest once more. 'Didn't I say this'd be fresh and flappin'?'

All eyes turned to the driftwood, where the duck had raised a wing. Two small fluffy bundles momentarily peeped out at the water.

'Those there eggs have been hatched,' Flake breathed. 'Saw and counted 'em two nights ago. Five luscious sweetmeats just waiting to be served up to us. More than enough for all, I reckon.'

A strange light was shining in his eyes, an infernal glitter that was more than the reflection of the street lamps shining down from the nearby road. It was the bloodlust, the thirst for slaughter that Jupiter put into the black hearts of all his followers.

To Fleabee's consternation, she saw the same fierce gleam appear in the eyes of the others, even Lickit.

'What about the mother, though?' Vinegar Pete asked warily. 'She's mighty big and I bet that beak of hers is real hard and sharp. I don't fancy that snapping at me! Break my spine real easy, she could. Risky business this is, very risky.'

Flake smacked the back of the rat's head. 'There's more than enough of us to bring her down,' he snarled. 'Us all got blades. All us need do is creep up real silent-like, then take her by surprise. She won't last five minutes, and think of the booty! Don't you fret about her beak, you won't be getting the bill for your take-away this night!'

'I doesn't like it,' Pete grumbled. 'What about the other one? Won't the proud dad be skulking about close by? We can't take on two of 'em.'

'There ain't no other duck,' Flake promised. 'That there mallard's a single mother. I been watching this happy family every night fer a week now and oh dear, I saw poor Mr Duck meet with an untimely end the other evening. Walked straight into a fox's jaws he did, the silly old quacker. That's why this job is so perfect and needs to be done tonight, before Foxy decides to make a return visit and put an early end to that widow's grief.'

'Ah,' muttered Rancid Alf in mock dismay. 'I couldn't bear the thought of that. Poor Mrs Ducky is just fox bait over there. Why, we'd be doing her and her little 'uns a mercy by scoffing them down here and now.'

Lickit was so filled with murderous delight that he licked his claws then slurped at the rubber of the tyre and patted his stomach greedily.

His uncle smiled but it was one of the most hideous sights Fleabee had ever seen. Then he put a claw to his cracked lips.

'Hush now,' he whispered. 'Let's be quieter than a gagged-up ghost what's lost his voice. Take yer lead from me and don't do nowt till I give the sign.' Brandishing his own jagged knife, he stepped silently from their cover.

Drawing their weapons, Leering Macky and Vinegar Pete stole after him. Rancid Alf glowered at his

daughter to do the same and stealthily followed.

Lickit ran his repulsive tongue over a steel spike that his late father had bequeathed him and then Fleabee was alone.

The ratgirl's legs felt weak and she leaned against the tyre. Panic was rising in her. The thought of what those fiends were about to do turned her stomach and the knife almost fell from her claws. The duck and her ducklings didn't stand a chance. The very thought of the impending massacre made her feel faint, and yet she was expected to take part.

'I can't,' she told herself.

Suddenly two fierce crimson points blazed back at her from the creeping black shapes of the departing rats and she knew that her father had glanced back to glare at her.

'But you're a rat, Fleabee,' she murmured wretchedly. 'This is what we do. You can't change it. Why do you think you're different? There's nothing special about you. Stop being so gutless, Scabmona wouldn't be dithering like this.'

And so Fleabee's small claws gripped the knife tightly and, taking a deep breath, she moved away from the tyre.

Not a sound disturbed the shore; it was as if the world had fallen silent just to witness this terrible crime. Even the water was hushed while it flowed slowly past, as if it, too, were watching and waiting.

Flake and the others sneaked ever closer to the driftwood nest.

Unaware of the terrible doom that crawled and inched its way towards her, the duck buried her head in her right wing, where three of her children were fidgeting and pressing as close to her as they could.

'Be still my speckled loves,' she told them. 'You will tire yourselves.'

'We're hungry Mamma!' they cried. 'Hungry and cold.'

'Shhh my little ones,' she soothed. 'In a short while we shall go dabbling for supper.'

'Where's Pappa? We want Pappa.'

'He has left us my dears, left us for good. Now be still.'

'Didn't he love us?'

The duck withdrew her head from her wing and gazed out across the creek. 'More than life,' she said, her yellow eyes dim and sad. 'More than life.'

Those clumsy, vulnerable hatchlings who burrowed into their mother's down and squabbled playfully with one another under her sheltering wings depended on her alone to feed and love them, and keep them from harm. It was all up to her now and she knew she would do anything to protect them.

Lost in sorrowful thoughts, she failed to see the dark shapes advancing from the left.

Over the grey mud the murderous rats picked their way, desperate not to betray their presence. The evil hunger that Jupiter had put into their black hearts was burning through their veins. They could almost taste the duck flesh in their slavering mouths.

Fleabee was shaking. She had never been more afraid or felt more helpless. There was no escape from this terrible nightmare. The nest was very close now, a few more steps and Flake would yell out and rush forward, knife raised to slash and stab.

She could see her father and the others tense, their heads lowered and their ragged ears flat against their skulls.

Sickened, the ratgirl shuddered.

Lickit's tongue was switching from side to side like a pink pendulum. Unlike Fleabee, he was trembling with excitement and couldn't wait to get his claws around a duckling's neck. His palms were sweaty and his taste buds were tingling with anticipation.

And then it happened.

He was so intent on the nest that was almost within reach, he did not see a glass bottle half-hidden in the mud. His fat feet stepped on it and the ratling slipped.

He gave a startled yell as his legs slithered under him and he toppled into the mud. He landed face down with a loud SMACK! and a SPLAT!

At once the duck quacked the alarm and pushed her frightened brood from the nest.

Flake shrieked in fury and rushed forward.

'Get her, lads!'

Slicing the air with his knife in great ferocious arcs, he lunged at the bird who stood at bay, shielding her children with wide, outstretched wings as they waddled frantically to the water.

The other rats charged at her but the mother stood her ground. Her beak shot out. Such was the unexpected violence of her defence that Flake was punched in the throat before he could strike any blow and Leering Macky was hurled aside as he tumbled backwards. Her powerful neck sprang back then swooped down again. This time the beak clamped tightly around Vinegar Pete's upraised arm and he was plucked from the ground.

Yowling, the sour-faced rat was catapulted through the air as she tossed her head and flung him away. Then she jerked her fierce yellow eyes back and rounded on Rancid Alf.

'Get gone from me, you feathery horror!' he cried, staggering up the bank. 'I wasn't gonna hurt you!'

Scrabbling backwards, his legs became tangled with his tail and he fell into the mud.

Like a monstrous dragon, the mallard reared over

him, her ominous shadow swamping his helpless form.

All he could do was stare up at her towering shape as she lifted her head high to deliver a fearsome blow with her beak.

Fleabee had watched all this in amazement. At first she had been relieved that the raid had gone disastrously wrong, but now a new terror seized her.

'No!' she yelled, hurrying to her father's side and throwing her arms about his neck. 'Don't hurt him!'

The duck turned its head and a golden eye shone down at her.

'He's my dad!' the ratgirl pleaded.

Rancid Alf covered his face, certain that this was the end of him. But to his astonishment nothing happened. Peering out between his claws he saw that a strange understanding, beyond the grasp of his mean cunning, had passed between his daughter and the mallard. The duck furled her wings and shook her tail, retreating back to the water.

'What happened?' Alf mumbled.

Fleabee smiled. 'She's done what she had to,' she explained. 'The ducklings are safe, that's what matters.'

Her father looked at her stupidly as though she had performed some impossible conjuring trick. 'I don't get you, Fleabee,' he said. 'Never have and never will.'

Flake meanwhile was nursing his throat but his rage

was worse than ever. Watching the duck withdraw, he sprang to his feet and in a rasping voice shrieked, 'There's still time! Don't let her get away – one last effort, lads!'

Leering Macky jumped to his side and, covered head to toe in mud, Lickit was suddenly there with his spike.

Vinegar Pete was feeling too sorry for himself to join them, but Rancid Alf threw off his daughter's protecting arms and leaped up.

'No!' Fleabee cried.

But her voice was lost, for the rats were already screaming bloody oaths. As one, they ran at the duck.

This time the mallard ran. Her children were safe and all the fight had left her. Over the shore her webbed feet went slapping and the rats came bounding after.

'Don't let her go!' Flake bawled. 'Rip her, rend her, tear her to fang-sized bites!'

Upon the glimmering water the five ducklings floated in a frightened group. They saw their beloved mother chased by those evil creatures and called out to her in high, piping cries.

The rats were almost upon her.

'Get her, boys!' the leader bellowed.

'Mother!' the ducklings quacked in distress.

Flake and the others thundered down the bank. The mallard's tail was so close it was almost tickling their snouts. They could feel the draught of the feathers on their greedy faces and Leering Macky reached out with a claw.

A dreadful squawk rent the night as he tore out a clump of feathers. The duck was panicking; she would never make it to the water. She could see her children watching and she despaired. What would become of them?

A foul, yodelling yell issued from Flake's throat as he launched himself into the air. On to the duck's back he pounced, gripping her shoulders with one claw while the other raised the knife to plunge into her neck.

But the shock of a rat landing on her back was the thing that saved her. Terrified, she threw open her wings and in an instant had left the ground. Up she flew, up over the creek. The buzzing street lamps of the nearby road dropped below her and the glittering sprawl of London stretched beneath in all directions.

Flake's knife dropped from his claw.

Screeching, he tried to hold on but it was no use.

From the mallard's back he fell, somersaulting through the air. The rats on the shore could only gawp. They saw his wriggling, flailing body plummet down and heard his woeful cries.

There was a mighty plop as Flake hit the water. They waited to see if he would surface.

'He were born lucky, an' no mistake,' Vinegar Pete grumbled, as he wandered over to join the rest. 'By rights he ought to be splattered on the ground. A puddle of jammy goo is what he should be.'

'He might be a goner yet,' Rancid Alf muttered. 'He could drown in that deep water if the fright hasn't already done him in.'

'Shouldn't you go after him?' Fleabee asked. 'It might not be too late. You could jump in and save him.'

Leering Macky gave a snort. 'Your girl's barmy,' he said.

Before anyone could say any more, a frenzied splashing erupted in the creek and Flake surfaced, gulping for air.

'Born lucky,' repeated Vinegar Pete in disgust.

Presently, a bedraggled and shaken Flake stumbled up the bank, coughing and retching. Doubling over he waited to catch his breath, then shook the water from his threadbare fur. When he saw Lickit he cuffed him about the head.

'This was all your fault!' he stormed. 'Us'd be stuffing our faces right now if you hadn't fell over! I'll not be bringing you on no more raids.'

A joyous quacking interrupted him and they all turned

to see the duck alight upon the water. Her ducklings shot towards her and they laughed and wept together.

'She looked like a stringy old bird anyways,' Flake spat. He stomped off, back to the embankment wall and the rusted pipe.

The others trudged along behind, feeling defeated and sorry for themselves. Lickit rubbed his head ruefully, pulling faces at his uncle's back. Vinegar Pete and Leering Macky were muttering to one another, while Rancid Alf was shaking his head in dismay.

'What'll my stringy old bird say?' he warbled.

Stooping to pick up the tail feathers that Leering Macky had discarded, Fleabee turned back and grinned at the duck and her offspring as they sailed serenely towards the river.

Then, taking one last yearning look at the stars, she followed the rest of the group into the pipe and returned to the sewers. But she would never be content to remain down there. She had seen the outside world and was determined to see more.

4

The Tale of 'Orace Baldmony

Klakkweena wasted no time in throwing Rancid Alf out of the rat hole. She would not listen to any of his explanations. He had returned empty-clawed and that was all she needed to know.

When her temper was roused she was a formidable adversary and after his efforts on the shore, the rat had no spare courage to contend with her.

Cursing, he slunk away, leaving Klakkweena to hurl a jumble of colourful abuse after him.

'You should've cracked him one,' Scabmona scolded her mother. 'And what about Fleabee? Ain't you going to chuck her out as well?'

Klakkweena gave her young daughter's spiky hair a sharp tug and the ratling squealed.

'Can't blame Fleabee for your dad's worthless idle bones,' she told her. "Sides, I want to know what happened out there, without him butting in with his daft lies.'

Fleabee had gone straight to her room to escape the inevitable argument, so Klakkweena barged in and demanded to know everything.

A short while later she and Scabmona were helpless with unkind laughter as the story of the bungled raid unfolded.

'So it were Lickit's fault,' the ratwife hooted. 'And that duck almost pecked Alf in half! Oh it's so like him, who else would get themselves in such a mess except him and his stupid cronies? What a useless bunch.'

'Why didn't you let him get bit?' Scabmona said crossly. 'I'd have cheered the bird on, I would've.'

Klakkweena wiped the callous tears from her eyes. 'And I'd give good fresh maggots to have seen the look on his face,' she chuckled. 'Serves him right, too.'

A small, stubby candle lit the cramped sleeping chamber. Its light was weak and guttering but Fleabee could see well enough to thread the feathers she had retrieved on to a strand.

Fleabee always liked to adorn herself with any odds and ends that took her fancy and in this, at least, she was no different from the other females of her kind. She already wore necklaces of pebble beads and two rings of copper wire pierced her left ear.

Her mother's cackles subsided. She and Scabmona were sitting on the messy pile of rags that served as Scabmona's bed, but Fleabee's was as neat and ordered as ripped scraps of tattered cloth could possibly be.

'Always better when it's just us three together,' the ratwife sighed. 'No Alf to get in our way.'

Fleabee pulled the new necklace over her head while Scabmona pulled something from her nose and nibbled it thoughtfully.

'Dad'll be back in the morning though,' the young ratgirl said. 'You always let him in again.'

Klakkweena shrugged. 'That'll depend on what he brings us. He'll be out there now rummaging and scrounging for summat to make up to me with. Well, if he know's what's good fer 'im he will be.'

Licking her bottom fang, she looked at Fleabee keenly and asked, 'So what did you make of the upper world, then?'

Her daughter hesitated before answering. If she sounded too enthusiastic they would laugh at her, so she merely said, 'It's very big.'

'Too much fresh air for me,' Klakkweena grunted. 'I never like goin' up top. Nasty, breezy place with flower smells and blousy colours – can't be healthy. Give me a dark, dirty, stagnant hole like this and I'm where I ought to be. You have to know where you belong.'

Fleabee smoothed down the feathers on her new necklace and wondered if she would ever find a place where she truly felt at home.

'Look what I got today,' Scabmona cried suddenly. Flinging heaps of rags aside she brought out a crudely sewn effigy of a rat made of sacking, with roughly stitched eyes and whiskers and a strip of chewed leather for a tail.

'A throttledoll,' Klakkweena observed, with a snort of approval. 'Oh the hours and hours I used to spend with mine when I was a ratling. The number of times I gave it a good walloping. Ha – the nasty torments I used to invent and inflict on it, oh – them were rum days!'

'Where did you get it?' Fleabee asked.

Scabmona held the doll tightly and twisted one of its legs. 'I swapped fer it,' she said.

'I wondered where Growler had got to.'

'I didn't swap him!' Scabmona answered hotly.

Fleabee could not imagine what else her sister owned. 'What then?' she asked.

Scabmona held up a small clenched fist. 'This!' she declared with a proud toss of her head that made the steeple of her hair judder. 'I gave that cry-baby Winjeela a lend of my knuckles for a few minutes.'

'That's a bad girl,' Klakkweena cackled.

'So where is Growler?' Fleabee persisted.

Her sister affected a yawn. 'He weren't scary enough,' she answered with a shrug. 'So I ate him.'

Holding the throttledoll upside-down, she wrung its neck. 'What was the horriblest thing you did to yours when you was little, Klakk?' she asked her mother.

The ratwife leaned back and stared up at the ceiling. She hardly ever thought about her childhood. The sputtering candlelight threw huge bouncing shadows over the rough walls and in the largest, darkest and most menacing of them, she could almost pick out the shape of her infamous father.

'Oh I did shockin' stuff,' she murmured. 'And all inspired by my dad. He used to tell such hackle-raising stories. Him being Jupiter's lieutenant before Morgan, he knew how to make my ears sing with fright, he did. Oh the threats and terrors he used to put on me, and how I'd take it out on my throttledoll after. Never did one of them things suffer more.'

She sighed and snatched the effigy from her daughter.

'Tell us one of them stories,' Scabmona pleaded. 'Tell us summat to make my claws pop out!'

Klakkweena hugged the doll to her chest for a moment, then a curious gleam kindled in her eyes and she looked across at Fleabee.

'Have you ever heard of 'Orace Baldmony?' she asked, promptly spitting on the floor at her mention of that name.

Scabmona kneeled forward. 'No!' she cried in excitement. 'Who's he? What did he do?'

''Orace Baldmony,' her mother continued, pausing only to spit a second time, 'was the only rat ever to have turned against his kind.'

'No!' Scabmona squealed, thrilled at the prospect of a juicy tale.

'Oh yes. Many years ago this was, way before I was born, or my dad or his great granddad, way way back. One of His Dark Highness's lackeys he were. A long time he served Him, but as the years went by, his backbone went soft. Some of the lovely wicked crimes his master ordered done, he dared have doubts about.'

'No!' Scabmona said again.

Klakkweena clucked with indignation.

'First of all he wouldn't lead the others on no jolly skirmishes,' she said tartly. 'Then he stopped sending them altogether and no one had proper meat for more time than is right for fang and heart. Turned yellow, he had. Didn't have the stomach for it no more. Someone should have blue-murdered him like Morgan did to my old dad, that's the only true way for a lieutenant of Jupiter to go, nice and violent. You can't have a rat not enjoy his proper sport, 'tain't natural.'

Fleabee shifted uneasily. Had her mother directed that last comment at her?

'So what happened to 'Orace then?' she asked.

At the mention of that name Klakkweena spat once more and Scabmona copied her.

'Crept away in the night,' the ratwife answered. 'Took himself off.'

'The dirty coward!' Scabmona yelled. 'He should've been strung up and gizzarded. An ordinary bloomer wasn't bad enough for the likes of him.'

Klakkweena agreed. 'Turned against the mighty Jupiter Himself,' she snarled. 'Filthy traitor. Off into the sewers he went, thinking he could escape the Great Lord's power – cracked old idiot!'

She stared at Fleabee, the flaring candle flame painting her frowning brows with shadow.

'No one can escape Him,' she said. 'From highest to lowest. No one gets away.'

'So what happened?' Scabmona shrieked impatiently.

'Through the tunnels that betrayer hurried and fled, until he stumbled on a broken Grille, a gateway to a cellar in the upper world – and guess what he discovers there?'

'A whole mouldy pie!' Scabmona crowed.

Klakkweena shook her head.

'Mice,' she told them.

'Even better! So did he peel them squeakers all at once and get really, really fat till he burst?'

'No.'

'Did he run 'em through an' roast 'em slow?'

'Not him.'

'Did he fry up their ears till they was crispy?'

'That's what you or me would do.'

Scabmona desperately wracked her brains to think what other gruesome tortures could be done to mice.

'I'll tell you what he did!' her mother snapped, as her temper swelled within her again. 'I'll tell you what that shameful, soap-livered piece of scum did with those mice – he made friends with them!'

She spat the final words in outrage and her children could only gape at her in stunned disbelief.

Scabmona's bottom lip began to tremble and for a moment it looked as though she was going to cry.

'That's foul!' she eventually managed to blurt out. 'It's disgusting! All them mouth-waterin' mouseys jumping about and him not even having so much as one itsy bitsy bite? But to go and be pals with such a tasty dinner ... It makes me want to throw up!'

Klakkweena returned the throttledoll to her and the ratling pummelled it with her fists. 'If this was him,' she said, 'I'd bloomer it and kick it and pull its head off!'

'And then?' Fleabee asked their mother. 'Did he stay there and live with them?'

An unpleasant smile fixed upon the ratwife's snout. 'He tried to,' she said. 'Tried to forget who an' what he was, but that's not possible. It ain't allowed, no matter how many silly songs them stupid mice sang round him and how many soppy dances they did. He was a rat, a rat of Deptford – and Jupiter, Lord of All, weren't going to let him get away with it – oh no.'

The gleam in her eyes sparkled more brightly. 'When Jupiter knew he'd scarpered, He gave orders that the traitor be found and if anyone was idiot enough to give him shelter, then they was to be dealt with as well. Everyone, from smallest ratling to the oldest fogy went howling and yammering through the sewers to hunt him down. Every hole, every slime pit was scoured and then they found it, that broken Grille.'

Enthralled, Scabmona started chewing the ear of her throttledoll but Fleabee looked down at her claws and avoided her mother's penetrating glance.

'Through that rusty hole our brave lads went screaming!' Klakkweena cried. 'That put a stop to the songs and skipping! How them mice wailed and tried to get away. A rare few managed it and I promise you, they never trusted no rat, not never again!'

'What about the others?' Scabmona asked, her mouth half-full of soggy ear.

'The others …' Klakkweena laughed softly. 'Our boys wasted no time. They went rushing at them, hacking and shredding till all them squeakers was robbed of their skins and a huge feast was had, best there's ever been. Then the Great Mighty Jupiter put a curse on that there Grille with His dark magic and, even to this day, any mousey who wanders too close to it gets lured in, down to the sewers. Down to His very own altar chamber they trot and He gulps 'em down.'

'And 'Orace Baldmony?' said Fleabee in a croaky whisper. 'What did they do to him?'

Her mother and sister spat in unison.

'He got what was coming!' Klakkweena growled. 'Pulled to pieces he was, and his mutinous head stuck on a spike as a warning to others who forget who and what they are.'

Scabmona cheered but a chill tingle ran up Fleabee's tail and she shivered.

'Wish I'd been there!' Scabmona said, giving the doll another thump. 'It's not fair – I can't wait to peel my first mousey!'

'How strong is Jupiter's magic?' Fleabee asked in a small, uncertain voice.

Klakkweena glanced quickly at Scabmona before making any answer. 'Don't you utter His name so freely,' she hissed. 'And don't you ask no questions like that neither. Knows everything, He does, look right into your heart He can, and read every secret thought in your head in a blinking moment!'

'Can He really?'

'Oh yes,' Klakkweena answered, her face contorting

at the unhappy memory. 'And when you stand in front of His altar and look up, up to the dark behind them candles, His eyes come embering out the blackness, sometimes red like blood, sometimes yellow as fire.'

'That's 'cos He has two heads!' Scabmona breathed in a solemn, awestruck voice. 'A two-headed hugeness what lives in the dark. Cor, I'd like to see that, I would. What's it like Ma, what's He like?'

Klakkweena stared into the wavering flame of their own humble candle and a look of pain twisted her ugly face.

'The first time,' she murmured. 'When those eyes seek you out. It's like your fur and skin falls off and there you are wearing only your bones and He's picking through your brains with His claws, scraping and digging down into the deepest bit of you, learnin' it all.'

Her voice trailed off and she put her head in her palms at the terrible memory.

Scabmona threw the throttledoll into the air and caught it between her sharp fangs. 'Can't wait!' she mumbled. 'Can't wait!'

'You're too young.' Fleabee told her.

Her sister gave the doll a vicious shake.

Klakkweena wiped her sweating palms on the rags that hung from her shoulders and rose from the bed.

'Scabmona is too young,' she agreed. 'But you ain't,

61

Fleabee. I meant to tell you before but Alf's barmy raid put it right out my head. First thing tomorrow, you've got to go to the altar chamber. Firstblood is in two nights' time and Morgan wants to see all the ratlings before then for the oath-taking.'

'The altar chamber?' Fleabee gasped. 'Where Jupiter lives?'

Klakkweena grinned. 'That's right. It's time you got stared at by them great fiery eyes. Let's see what His Unholy Darkness makes of you, 'cos Alf and me got no idea what kind of rat you are.'

Extinguishing the candle with a flick of her claw, the ratwife left the sleeping chamber.

Fleabee lay back on her bed. She should have expected this. There had been rumours flying around the tunnels that Morgan always gave the ratlings a fierce talking-to before Firstblood and that they had to swear allegiance to Jupiter. But she had not listened to them.

The night had already been filled with fear and now there was this new dread to face. What would the terrible Jupiter do to her, if He looked inside her heart and found it to be gentle and loving?

Fleabee was glad that the room was now in darkness and her sister could not see the tears trickling down her furry face.

Yet Scabmona was still chuckling.

5

Before the Dark Portal

'U p you get!' Klakkweena's harsh yell jolted Fleabee from the troubled sleep she had finally fallen into.

The ratgirl rubbed her eyes and stretched.

'You're going to Morgan!' her mother reminded her. 'You don't want to draw his bile by being late. He'd like that, he would, but I won't have it.'

Fleabee brushed the hair from her eyes and hastily made her bed. Klakkweena looked on with disgust, then stomped out.

From her untidy corner, Scabmona grumbled in her sleep. 'Hope Jupiter eats you,' she said sleepily. 'With both his heads.'

Fleabee followed Klakkweena into the main chamber. A collection of dry and mould-spotted bread crusts were stacked against the wall.

'Dad been back, then?' she asked.

'He has, but it'll take more than stale pickings like that for him to worm his way inside here. I slung him out again and told the ugly sot he'd best not show his wonky face again till he's got summat a whole lot better!'

In spite of her sneering words, Klakkweena broke off a large corner of the hard bread and wolfed it greedily.

'Shake yerself and get gone,' she warned her daughter, amid a spray of crumbs. 'The other ratlings are already on their way.'

Taking a chunk of bread for herself, Fleabee crunched her teeth into it.

'What will Jupiter do to me?' she asked nervously.

'Shrivel you from your toenails up if you don't get a move on!'

With her tail dragging behind her, Fleabee left the rat hole.

Klakkweena leaned against the entrance and watched her daughter trudge along the ledge.

'If Morgan and Himself can't sort her out,' she muttered under her breath, 'there's no hope for the sorry wretch.'

As Fleabee disappeared around the corner Klakkweena glanced up and down the tunnel. Other sharp faces were peering out of their holes that morning. There was nothing unusual in that, but today the atmosphere was charged with an air of expectance and anxiety.

'So our Fleabee's not the only one,' she said, her brows twitching with interest.

Slipping back into the hole, she discovered Scabmona stuffing her face with stale bread and all thoughts of her other daughter were instantly forgotten as she chased her out.

'Scarper – you greedy, balloon-bellied blowfly!' she shrieked.

The altar chamber of Jupiter, Lord of All, was not far. Only three tunnels separated it from where Fleabee and the other rats lived, but she had never dared venture into that unholy place.

To be summoned to stand before Jupiter was every rat's darkest fear. Only Morgan had leave to come and go as he pleased. To trespass in that chamber meant instant death.

The fact that Fleabee had been instructed to go did nothing to quell the terrors that flared inside her. As she drew closer to a small passageway that branched from the main tunnel, she took a deep, steadying breath and bit her bottom lip.

She knew this led directly to the altar chamber. Her father had pointed it out to her often enough and bowed low whenever they passed. An unnatural blackness filled this cramped and narrow way. It was darker in there than any deep sewer night she had ever known.

The ratgirl wondered if Jupiter had woven enchantments across the threshold to keep out all but the most determined. She wished that she had not been late. To step into that mysterious darkness in the company of others would not have been so frightening, but to go into it alone made her scalp tingle and her whiskers wilt.

Moments of indecision crawled by and she pressed her claws to her mouth. The longer she remained out there the worse it became; every instant she stayed away from the gathering pushed her deeper into trouble.

'Stop dithering!' an impatient voice snapped behind her.

Startled, Fleabee leaped up and spun around.

Scabmona had crept up after her and was standing there with arms folded and the throttledoll crushed to her chest.

'What are you doing here?' Fleabee asked in a croaky whisper. 'You can't come in!'

Scabmona waggled the doll in her face. 'I only want a look,' she cried, not caring that her voice was echoing through the tunnel. 'I'm not waiting till the time of my Firstblood, I wanna see that two-headed horror right now!'

'Go home!' Fleabee commanded.

'Oh chew on a poisoned brick!' came the retort. 'I'm not goin' nowhere. His Nibs won't see me, I'll stay well tucked inside this 'ere passage and keep my trap shut. No one will know I'm even there, unless you squeal on me.'

Fleabee could tell there was no arguing with her. Besides, she was secretly glad to have her sister there.

And so, together, they pressed into the midnight-black passageway. Fumbling blindly in the dark, they stubbed their toes on invisible stones and grazed their outstretched palms on the rough, sharp walls that hemmed them in. The route was not a straight one. It twisted and dipped so not a glimpse of the end was in sight till the very last turn was made and then they saw it – the Chamber of Jupiter.

This was one of the oldest parts of the sewers: a wide, high space with numerous openings leading off in different directions, on many levels. Deep, foaming water churned far below; above, the curving walls converged in lofty, gothic arches, vanishing up into a swirling gloom that floated overhead. A chaotic tangle of rusted chains plunged and looped out of that murky canopy like the thirsty roots of a huge metal tree, forming a ceiling choked with iron nooses and crazy chandeliers.

Dominating all this was a single, great portal built into the main wall.

When Fleabee saw it, she caught her breath and reached for Scabmona's claw.

In that shadow-filled place, for hundreds of years, Jupiter the Lord of the Sewers had dwelt.

Fleabee thought that it looked like the wailing mouth of some monstrous creature. Deep down that cavernous throat, all the horror and despair was born. Evil flowed from it in unseen waves, spilling out into the tunnels to burden the hearts of Jupiter's subjects. She could almost feel the malice pour past her ankles and even Scabmona gave her claw a fearful squeeze.

But there was no turning back now.

Standing either side of the portal, two large candles burned steadily; yet even their bright flames could not illumine the shadows that Jupiter wrapped about Himself. Between those candles, upon a ledge was seated every ratling due to take part in the festival of Firstblood and striding amongst them was Morgan – Jupiter's lieutenant.

A snarl was on his lips as he glowered and bullied his way through. Fleabee knew all of them by sight and most by name. From the scowl on his pinched snout, she could tell that Morgan was not impressed.

Occasionally he would stoop to inspect a scar or pull on an ear, but he would always push the ratlings away with a threat and a jeer. He was a piebald, Cornish rat with a stumpy tail, whose back and shoulders had slid into a perpetual hunch due to his many years of fawning service. He knew every low trick and nothing got past him.

Tottering behind him, carrying a large tattered book, with a bottle of ink hung around his neck and his greasy hair stuck with many quills, was a short shrew-like rat with a long snout and tiny bright eyes. Blots and smudges of ink stained his mouth where he absently sucked his quills, and his claws were like mottled mittens.

Wormy Ned was one of the few who could read and write. He kept records of all the important pronouncements and new laws and set down the ever-changing rules of Ratiquette. Every rat who lived in the sewers had an entry in that book. Under their names was scrawled their sins and fears, favourite bribes, what spiteful rumours were muttered against them and the most effective method of blackmailing them.

Nobody liked Wormy Ned's book and they liked him even less.

Reaching the edge of the assembled ratlings, Morgan turned on his heel and marched through them again. Wormy Ned whisked about and did the same.

While their bony backs were turned, Fleabee took her chance. Whispering to Scabmona to remain hidden, she tiptoed out and hurried to join the others.

But little escaped Morgan's attention – certainly not a plump ratgirl late for a summons.

'So honoured you could grace us with your presence!' he said abruptly, without even turning to look at her. 'No doubt there was some dire emergency which prevented you being here at the time appointed.'

Fleabee sat down with a jolt and blinked in surprise and fear.

'We're all waiting,' Morgan continued, still with his back to her. 'Tell us of this woeful calamity.'

There was a terrible pause. Everyone except Morgan

turned to look at the ratgirl. Wormy Ned peered hard at her, then licked a claw and turned purposefully to the back pages of his book.

'Well?' Morgan said. 'The only rat I let hold his tongue is Big Smiler and that's 'cos I cut his lips off when he were a lad and now he spits worse than a gushing drain when he speaks.'

Fleabee wrung her claws. 'I'm sorry!' she apologised. 'I didn't mean to be late – I really didn't!'

Very slowly Morgan turned to face her.

'Sorry?' he repeated. 'What sort of milksop bleating is that?'

He signalled to Wormy Ned and the short rat promptly read out: 'Fleabee, eldest of Rancid Alf's litter, nothing else set down against her – except the usual.'

Morgan's hatchet face lit up, a ghastly grin appeared across his snout and he prowled a little closer.

'One of Alf's litter, is you?' he said. 'So that venomous stickleback, Klakkweena, is your mother.'

Fleabee nodded, feeling extremely uncomfortable under his piercing scrutiny.

'Then this is the grandchild of Black Ratchet!' he snorted, bringing his face close to hers. 'The wickedest old sinner what ever gasped, he was. Good job I did fer him, would've broke his flinty heart to see how weak and sappy his scurvy brood ended. What throbs and pulses in your veins then? Nowt but muddy water from

71

the looks of it – I'll wager it ain't as scarlet and steamin' as what pumped through his.'

Morgan licked his yellow fangs at the memory, then pulled away.

Fleabee shivered while, concealed in the shadows of the passageway, Scabmona had a face like thunder and was torturing the throttledoll, pretending it was Morgan.

'But you're all a wishy-washy, pitiful tribe of runts,' the Cornish rat shouted. 'I can't recall a more timid, cowardly-looking crew. What use do you think you'll be to Our High and Awful Majesty? Not much, I reckon!'

His disapproving gaze roved over them all. 'Why, there's not even a dozen killers among you,' he spat. 'And one of them did it by accident.'

He looked at Wormy Ned for confirmation.

'Toadface Billy,' Ned announced, consulting the book. 'Claimed he blue-murdered Joey the Giblet but it was a lucky trip and a handy-placed nail, nothing to be proud of there. His account is still very much in the red and wanting.'

The ratling called Toadface Billy hung his large and ugly head.

Morgan pointed a shaming claw at him, then told Wormy Ned to continue. 'List 'em all,' he commanded. 'Let's hear who's yet to prove themselves. Let's hear who's got only two more days till the night of Firstblood.'

'Erbert the Stink,' Ned began. 'The aforementioned Fleabee, Croaknelly, Clarty Jim, Snub-Nosed Charlie, Wallowart, Fleurcanker, Maungewickit, Viralmyra, Smutty Bob, Mildew, Pigmince Larry, Hoggerna, the aforementioned Toadface Billy, Spoiler, Rattanna, Twisted Sid, Rumpleclout and Lickit.'

Hearing that last name Fleabee looked up in surprise. She had seen Lickit among the assembly and had avoided sitting anywhere near him. He was such a naturally horrible creature that this news came as a complete shock to her.

Flake's nephew was too busy running his repulsively long tongue over the candle wax to register even the slightest flicker of embarrassment or disgrace.

'Hark at that,' Morgan cried at them all. 'Was there ever such a tally of craven, yellow-bellied wasters?'

'Never!' Wormy Ned replied with a stern shake of

the head. 'Not in all my registers and records, I done never seen such a dismal accounting. It's a downright tragic total loss, that's what it is.'

'A worry to be sure,' Morgan agreed, lowering his voice and pushing his way through to stand between the candles. 'But there's still time, yes ... still time and who are we to judge? This limp rabble may prove us wrong yet. Who knows? Maybe, sitting in this lot, there's one who'll do fer me some day and take my place? Who knows?'

A buzz of excitement began as the ratlings considered this and greatly relished the possibility.

Morgan permitted them several moments of enjoyment then clapped his claws for silence. 'It'll take more guts and wits than what any of you sloppy sparrows own to finish me!' he barked, his stumpy tail flicking from side to side. 'The rat ain't yet born who could take me on so don't get any uppity ideas, 'cos I'm a villain what can scare the very skeleton out of you!'

In the passageway, Scabmona had exhausted all her torments and the throttledoll lay forlorn and stamped upon, next to her on the ground.

'I'll bloomer you,' she whispered. 'I'll bloomer and doofer you – just see if I don't.'

But between the candles, Morgan had grown solemn and she crossed her arms and attended to what he was saying.

'The hour has come,' he declared. 'The hour when you swear your allegiance to Him what you owe everything to, Him what never sleeps, Him what seeds the harvest of death and hate in us all, Him what lives and never dies. Stand and bow down before His Dark Glory!'

The ratlings whimpered but rose slowly and lifted their unhappy snouts to the blackness within the arched portal before them. Lickit rolled his tongue into his mouth and kept it safe behind his teeth.

'Oh Great Gruesomeness!' Morgan yelled. 'Come forth, come view this miserable crop of young whelps. Come bestow a drop of Your limitless wicked bliss into their quivering hearts!'

Fleabee shuffled nervously but in the passageway Scabmona had jumped to her feet and was beaming from ear to ear with glee.

'The two-headed monster's on his way!' she gurgled to herself. 'Devilish, devilish! Cor – what a battering – what a scalding!'

Wormy Ned closed his book and bowed so low that the ink bottle about his neck clinked on the brick ledge beneath his feet.

No one noticed. The ratlings' attention was fixed solely upon the darkness and they waited with their hearts pounding.

Suddenly a breath of foul-smelling air blew against

their faces. It grew stronger, gusting about the chamber till the chains rattled overhead and the candle flames buckled and bent, yet they were not extinguished. Someone uttered a gasp of fear and Fleabee was not the only one who wanted to run away.

Jupiter was approaching.

From the depths of his ancient, night-filled lair the God of the Rats came.

At first they could only hear the deep, resonant breathing of some gargantuan beast, then two points of golden fire crackled open in the distant dark and steadily burned their way closer.

It was too much for a young ratgirl called Wallowart. She fell on her knees and stopped up her ears. Fleabee would have done the same but she was too afraid to move.

'Prince of Blight and Horror!' Morgan greeted. 'Supreme Spirit of Shade and Sorrow, see these dainty let-downs and inspire them with Your deadly power!'

At once the candles sparked and spat, the flames blazed fiercely and stretched up into the foggy gloom above. The eyes within the portal advanced and their brutal glare liquefied the knees of the assembled ratlings and each one of them collapsed to join Wallowart on the ground.

In the passageway even Scabmona felt the malevolent force of Jupiter's presence. Cowering back, she covered her face with the throttledoll and, for the first time in her life, began to sob.

'My Lord!' Morgan grovelled. 'We who are unworthy thank You for the honour of granting this audience.'

The great, shining eyes turned on him and, in a booming powerful voice that shook the very ledge, Jupiter spoke.

'Faithful Morgan,' He said. 'So, another year has crumbled away. And the time of the fealty oath is upon us once more.'

'Yes, O Commander of Sinister Forces! But these are a poor and pasty-looking bunch of chalk-spined idlers. I humbly crave Your forgiveness in showing them to You.'

The fiery eyes stared down at the petrified ratlings and a mocking tone crept into Jupiter's voice.

'A quailing crew, admittedly,' He said. 'Yet with my arts I can blow life into the cinders of their valour and kindle the raging nature that sleeps within their breasts. Bid them rise.'

Morgan yelled for the ratlings to stand but they were still too afraid, so he kicked and tore at them until at last they were on their feet once more, trembling in despair.

'Now heed what Our Wicked Magnificence has to tell you,' he snarled, thumping those nearest to him. 'Or you'll go serve Our Master on the other side of the candles!'

'Peace!' Jupiter commanded. 'Do not threaten them.'

Morgan jumped as though stung and bowed instantly. 'Forgive me, O Dark Divinity!' he implored.

'These are the children of my beloved realm,' Jupiter declared. 'Though they are weak and afraid, they are in my care and I love each of them dearly. Yet weakness can be turned to strength and fear to anger and anger to hatred. Thus shall it be with these, my smallest treasures.'

The fiery eyes retreated into the shadows. There was a silence in which only the anxious breaths of the ratlings could be heard, and then a second pair of eyes came flaming from the darkness. As crimson fires they shone and the malice that fuelled them made Fleabee feel faint. The youngsters around her murmured unhappily and uttered small cries.

Suddenly the candles spluttered and everyone covered their heads as the bright yellow flames fizzled, then roared. With a rush of ruby light, they turned a violent, bloody red and the chamber was engulfed in an infernal glare.

Stricken with terror, Scabmona cursed herself for following her sister and there, in the shadows of the passageway, the little ratgirl wet herself.

'I am Jupiter!' roared the voice. 'It is my thought that guides you, my hate that feeds you, my will that scorches you. Swear unto me your undying devotion, swear unto me an allegiance that will bear you to everlasting strife and discord, swear unto me your very souls!'

From the blazing candle flames a ruddy smoke rose, curling up into the gloom above, then drifted down through the chains to fill the chamber with a dense scarlet fog.

'Put your claws to your throats.' Jupiter commanded.

The ratlings obeyed. They knew it was the pledging gesture, but they were distressed to see the eerie mist creep over the ledge and spiral up around their legs.

The crimson eyes flashed in the portal and with that, their fears were forgotten.

Every ratling froze and all expression drained from their faces. The hellish light of Jupiter's malevolent eyes transfixed them.

Fleabee felt numb. The choking smoke wreathed and twined about her, seeping into her nose and mouth, but she did not care.

The eyes of Jupiter were like spinning globes of intense red flame and she could not tear her gaze away. Everything she was, her doubts, her secret wishes and innermost thoughts were dislodged and cast aside. All that mattered was the conquering desire to praise the God of the Sewers and do whatever He instructed.

'Who am I?' His voice called out inside her head.

'Jupiter!' Fleabee answered, her impassioned cry

adding to the chorus of her fellow ratlings.

'What am I?' Jupiter demanded.

'Our Lord!' they yelled in unison. 'Our Mighty Tyrant and Protector!'

'What are you?'

'We are nothing – worthless servants!' they shouted. 'Yours to command!'

'Will you die for me?'

'Yes!'

The eyes blazed brighter, filling the ratlings' vision. To them there was nothing else in the whole world, just the furious, savage splendour of those twin demonic suns.

Harsh laughter echoed within the portal and when Jupiter spoke again, it was in a repellent, loathsome whisper.

'Will you … kill for me?' He asked.

The eyes of the ratlings began to shine with a light of their own. The radiance that glittered there welled up from within their own selves and with it came a terrible, boiling hatred and barbarism – the bloodlust.

'Yes!' they yammered. 'YES!'

'Obey only me,' Jupiter bellowed. 'Crush all who would oppose me.'

The ratlings held out their claws and jumped up and down ecstatically.

'Jupiter!' they screamed. 'Mighty Jupiter! Anything! Anything!'

Jupiter laughed once more and the crimson eyes retreated into the shadows.

'So be it,' He said and the eyes were lost in the darkness.

The candle flames burned yellow again and the smoke returned to a meandering black thread that vanished overhead.

Morgan fanned the thinning red fog away from his face and sniggered.

'He knows how to get the little vermin worked up,' he said to Wormy Ned.

The other rat grinned. 'Does the same for the big vermin as well,' he agreed, taking a quill from his greasy hair and dipping it into the ink bottle. 'Never failed yet,' he continued, scratchily recording the morning's events in the book. 'They might turn out to be a real bad bunch after all. You'd best look to them though – you know what they're like when they're fresh and fierce. Liable to do all sorts of madness.'

Morgan stared at the ratlings. The wild light was still glittering in their eyes. Some were already squabbling with one another and Twisted Sid and Snub-Nosed Charlie were rolling on the ground, locked in a deadly fight. Wallowart was even trying to scale the upper ledge so she could go running after Jupiter in the dark.

The Cornish rat waded into them, pulled the two

combatants apart and dragged Wallowart from the bricks.

'I'll have none of that!' he snapped, delivering blows to several heads, then knocking two more together. 'This ain't no place for brawling. Take it outside and prepare yourselves for Firstblood.'

The ratlings mumbled rebelliously. Pigmince Larry bared his fangs at Morgan, but a sharp shove in the belly sent the youngster rolling backwards.

'They always think they're lions!' Morgan chuckled to Wormy Ned. 'Go on, get out of it the lot of you! Before I trim some ears.'

Squealing and snarling, the rabble rushed along the ledge towards the passageway. Fleabee ran with them, her mind in chaos. Voices were baying for blood around her and she laughed when she realised that one of those voices was her own.

'Does your heart good to see the change in them little beggars,' Morgan cackled.

Wormy Ned sucked the end of his quill thoughtfully. 'It's moments like that what makes this poxy life worth the struggle,' he mused.

'Don't talk wet,' Morgan scorned him. 'It's the power and the slaughter what does that.'

'Oh yes,' Ned sniggered.

Into the passage the ratlings charged. Their brutal spirits were high and they jostled and pushed one

another in that narrow way. Fleurcanker tripped and Viralmyra fell on top of her. Every ratling bumped against the one in front and in moments they were all wriggling on the floor in a confused and tangled scrum.

Terrible shouts and screeches rang out as they struggled to free their tails and legs from those of their neighbours. Then, issuing a blood-curdling scream, a small squat shape came leaping from the shadows and dived straight into the middle of the knotted bodies. Scabmona's eyes were gleaming in the dark. She had sworn herself to Jupiter just as the others had done. Now, desperate to fight and bite anything that came her way, she pounced on the first tail that flailed and jiggled in front of her face, seized it in her claws and sank her teeth into it.

Lickit yowled in pain and shot upwards, scrambling over the floundering ratlings to race out into the larger tunnel beyond.

Still clutching hold of his tail, Scabmona bit it a second time.

Lickit whirled around and snatched it from her jaws and her grasp.

Furiously he rounded on her, his long tongue flicking out like that of a snake.

'I'm going to thpike you here and now!' he lisped.

'Bring it on, ratboy!' she answered, bouncing up and down and brandishing the throttledoll, while blowing a sharp raspberry. 'I heard Stumpy-drawers in there, you ain't never doofered anyone before – think you can bloomer me, do you? Dream on, dribbler!'

With the steel point raised above his head, Lickit barged forward. Scabmona darted nimbly aside and he went blundering into the wall.

'Haw haw!' she taunted. 'I ducked!' More laughter. 'Yes – I heard how you wrecked that plunder raid. You couldn't skewer a dead duck, never mind a live one.'

A determined growl rumbled in Lickit's throat and he drew the weapon over his glistening tongue. 'You'll be called Kebabmona in a minute!' he promised.

But in the passageway the other ratlings had extricated themselves from the sprawl and even as Lickit made to rush at her, they came surging out, spilling on to the ledge, driving them apart and separating them completely.

The fight that had started in the altar chamber

between Twisted Sid and Snub-Nosed Charlie erupted once more. They tore at each other's hair then threw one another against the brickwork, crashing into anyone in their path. More scuffles and fights broke out and Scabmona flung herself into them, lashing out with her little fists to shove the ratlings aside so she could reach Lickit.

'Out of my way!' she cried. 'Lemme at him! Lemme at him!'

Suddenly her feet left the ground and she was swept up into the air.

'Put me down!' she shrieked, kicking and flailing her arms. 'Put me down!'

Fleabee had battled her way out of the warring ratlings and had pulled her sister clear of them.

'I want to bite his tail off!' Scabmona howled. 'I want to doofer him!'

'You'll doofer no one!' Fleabee fumed. 'You're going straight home!'

Scabmona struggled and wrestled. 'Can't make me!' she cried, repeatedly hitting her sister with the throttledoll. 'Won't go!'

And she kicked and scratched and wriggled so viciously that she slipped out of Fleabee's arms and hared off up the tunnel, away from the fighting.

'Come back!' Fleabee yelled, exasperated. 'Where are you going now?'

Scabmona performed a little dance. 'I'm going to go hunt me a mousey!' she sang. 'And when I catch one I'm gonna peel him good and proper. So long – soppy sister!'

With a wave and a high hooting laugh, she raced ahead and hurtled around the first corner.

Fleabee called after her but Jupiter's power still burned in her veins and for the first time she, too, wondered what a freshly-skinned mouse would taste like.

'Wait for me!' she shouted urgently. 'I'm coming with you! We'll peel them together!'

And she ran through the sewers, licking her lips as her eyes shone a fierce crimson.

6

Trespassers in the Cellar

Through the great tunnels the sisters hurried. Scabmona was incredibly speedy for her short legs and continually bounded far ahead of Fleabee. At times the distance between them was so great that she was lost from sight completely, but her wild laughter always betrayed which path she had taken.

Still caught up in the consuming fervour of the oath-taking, Fleabee followed. Darting up sloping paths, scrambling across broken ledges and leaping over fallen pipes, they ran. Along waterways that neither of them had ever ventured down, they hurried – heedless of where they were going.

To find a mouse was uppermost in their minds and, as they had never encountered such a creature before,

their hope was to discover
new territories where those squeaking
mouthfuls might be found.

So fierce and overwhelming was the craving that the morning wore on without their realising how long they had journeyed. Jupiter's words inspired a supernatural vigour that carried them further than would have been possible before.

Into a sewer where many openings branched off in different directions, Fleabee finally paused and drew long, gulping breaths.

Scabmona was already capering along the ledge some way in front, peering into the dark, cave-like passages and sniffing the air, deciding which of them to choose.

Refreshed, Fleabee was about to chase after her when

a movement of air ruffled the fur on her cheek and, curious, she turned.

Close by, a large panel of rotted wood leaned against the wall. The sewers were full of flotsam but there was something unusual about this – it seemed to be placed there for a purpose.

The ratgirl moved towards it and the draught blew more strongly on her face, wafting the hair from her eyes.

Looking closely, she saw that strange drawings had been scrawled across the warped and mouldering surface: weird charms and mysterious symbols and letters that she was unable to read.

Fleabee reached out a claw. The wood was ancient, and over the long years, damp had crept into every fibre of its grain. In places it had completely disintegrated, and through these ragged gaps the air currents were blowing.

'What's it hiding back there?' she wondered to herself. 'A route to the big outside? Maybe this is to stop something coming down here?'

Cautiously, she tried to push the barricade aside. At her touch, it buckled and collapsed, crumbling softly in her claws like a wet biscuit. Over the ledge the soggy, flaking splinters went toppling and splashed loudly in the water below.

Fleabee stared at what had been revealed, and blinked. There in the sewer wall was a square opening. A steadily rising shaft lay beyond and, when she crouched down to gaze up it, a gust of warm air swirled past her.

The shaft was not very long. At the far end she could clearly see pale patterns of light glowing on dusty bricks.

Intrigued, Fleabee climbed inside and, stooping slightly beneath the low ceiling, made her way upward.

Presently the faint beams fell across her. They were streaming through a barrier of scrolling ironwork, ornately wrought in the shape of fern leaves. Pushing her snout through the spaces, she stared at the world beyond.

A vast shadowy room stretched out before her. The one grimy window built high into a wall filtered a feeble stream of daylight from the street above, casting a dim radiance over the discarded lumber which crammed the enormous place.

Huge boxes and immense crates loomed all around, forming sheer ravines that rose from the foothills of old newspaper heaps. A pyramid of dented tins streaked with drab paint was stacked nearby, surrounded by fallen pillars of unused wallpaper. Mops and brushes on long poles leaned this way and that, creating giant diagonals that sliced through the weak, angled rays. Their shadows threw black bars over Fleabee's face, in which her eyes sparkled with a cruel, scarlet light.

The ratgirl was looking into a cellar, and she realised with a callous laugh that the rotted barricade below had been put there to keep rats like her from finding this place.

Standing back, she saw that one corner of the ironwork had rusted away and she could crawl through very easily.

'It's the Grille!' she exclaimed. 'The one Mother spoke about.'

The awful light burned more fiercely in her eyes. 'There are mouseys through there,' she murmured. 'Plump, tender mouseys.'

As if in a trance, she ducked and crossed from the sewer realm – into the upper world.

The warmer air of the cellar wrapped around her, and for several moments the ratgirl stood in the striped sunlight wondering where to find the nearest mouse.

'What made that splash?' Scabmona's voice echoed from behind. 'Did you fall in and drown? You big hefty lump!'

Fleabee turned as her sister's footsteps scampered up the shaft and she shot through the Grille in an instant.

'Mangle me sideways!' she exclaimed, staring round open-mouthed. 'Look at this place, just goggle at it!'

Scabmona was not one to waste any time drinking in the sunlight. She immediately ran at two great boxes covered in colourful scrawl and dived through a hole cut into one of them.

'What's all this?' she shrieked, as she emerged dragging garlands of paper decorations behind her.

They were painted to resemble leaves and blossom. Pulling a disgusted face, she blew her nose on a flower to show her contempt, then ripped up several more.

'Useless tat!' she sneered, before jumping into the second large box.

They were the boxes that the mice, who lived in the Skirtings and Landings of this empty old house, used in their great Spring ceremony. These were the chambers of Summer and Winter which they hauled from the cellar every year and it was in these that the young mice were given their mousebrasses.

The two ratgirls knew nothing about this however. The beliefs of mice had never been mentioned in their squalid hole. Their parents, like every other rat, were only interested in the best way to eat them.

Loud bumps and rustles sounded within the Chamber of Winter, accompanied by scornful grunts. Then Scabmona tittered and came bustling out, holding a paper ghost in front of her.

'Wooooooooooo!' she wailed, flapping the wobbly arms and trying to sound as hollow and frightening as possible. 'I'm a dead mousey. I been peeled and chopped into rashers. My bloomered carcass is in Scabmona's belly. Ooooooooh, she's a cruel enemy and the brutalist fighter what ever came rampaging!'

Emitting a final gurgling howl, she threw the ghost at her sister then nipped back into the box, fetching out an armful of other gruesome-looking things.

'There's masks and cut-out skellingtons,' the ratgirl laughed. 'Who put them here? What do you reckon they're for? There's a big awful head painted in there as well with huge teeth. Its mouth opens and shuts – real nasty. What a find! I'm gonna take these back for Firstblood.'

Throwing her swag to the ground she fished out a particularly hideous blue and silver mask and held it to her face, staring through the great eye holes.

Fleabee looked at her sister in puzzlement. She had never seen Scabmona merely playing before – there was usually some malicious plan behind everything she did.

'I'm gonna doofer that Lickit,' Scabmona warbled, a shadow of her normal self creeping back. 'He'll take a running jump when he sees me in this!'

'You don't know where we are, do you?' Fleabee said. 'You haven't realised.'

'Realised what? You know, I'm thinking of starting up a gang. I want to call us 'The Slay 'em Slow Six' but it might have to be 'The Fump 'em in the Froat Five' if Winjeela's still in a sulk.'

Fleabee traced her claws over the ironwork of the Grille. 'Look at it,' she said. 'Don't you remember the story?'

Still staring through the mask, Scabmona frowned. She could not understand what her sister meant. The scrolling leaves of the Grille signified nothing to her young mind, but then she stared at the surrounding wall. There were pictures drawn there, strange symbols similar to the ones that covered the wooden panel she had failed to notice before. The words and letters were just meaningless squiggles to her, but here and there were images of frightened mice depicted running away from dark shapes. Suddenly it all made sense.

But in that same instant, when she realised where she was, and before she could cry out for joy, a different sound began and the explosion of delight stalled in her throat.

Outside the cellar, up the high steps at the other end of the dusty gloomy room, beyond the immense closed door, there were voices.

Scabmona turned slowly and Fleabee reached out to hold her claw.

The voices were high and filled with merry laughter.

'Mouseys!' Scabmona breathed, and a tear of happiness welled up in her eye.

Behind the ratlings the shadows about the Grille seemed to deepen, as if the very sound of the mice was enough to stir the spells that Jupiter had placed upon it. With a drizzle of falling rust, an iron frond unfurled and the dark curse awakened.

Fleabee could almost hear Jupiter's voice trumpeting in her ears once more and her fear and devotion to Him swelled to new heights.

'How many do you think there are out there?' she uttered hoarsely.

Scabmona shook her head. The sound was a blend of many voices, some singing, some laughing, others chattering.

'Plenty,' she said, rubbing her stomach.

'Wish I still had Dad's knife,' Fleabee whispered.

Scabmona sniggered. 'We got claws and fangs,' she declared. 'We'll get enough with them, don't you worry.'

'Yes, you're right. They're only puny mouseys, what chance do they stand against us?'

Scabmona's eyes flashed in the gloom. 'None! We're rats of Deptford!'

'Then let's do what we're known for!' Fleabee cackled. 'Let's rush them and take down as many as we can.'

With the bloodlust burning fiercely in their veins, the sisters moved forward, their minds consumed with hatred and murder. Behind them the ironwork of the Grille writhed and squirmed like serpents, as the power of Jupiter poured out from it.

But a string of decorations had snagged around Scabmona's ankle. The ratgirl was oblivious to it until it grew taut, and then she gave her leg a violent yank. The string broke, but so forcefully had she pulled on it that the Chamber of Winter came toppling over.

There was a juddering crash. Paper ghosts flew into the air; a barrage of masks went soaring over their heads like avenging kites and streamers rained down in a thick blizzard of colour.

A stack of sticks and rods slid to the floor with a

clatter and the ratlings stared anxiously at the huge door at the top of the steps. Had the mice heard?

Long moments passed. The ghosts fluttered down and the streamers settled on top of them. A pink ribbon landed across Scabmona's ears, trailing over her snout, but she was listening too intently to care.

The cheerful noises were still drifting through the door and the ratgirls breathed a sigh of relief. The mice still did not know they were there.

'Would've made it a lot tougher if we had to go looking for them!' Scabmona said.

'Let's do this quick then,' Fleabee urged. 'I want to hear them squeal and see the looks of terror on their faces!'

Scabmona nodded but, casting her glance around the devastation she had caused, she saw something that held her attention.

'Hang on,' she cried. 'What's that?'

Where the Chamber of Winter had stood, there was a large round lid of a biscuit tin that bore an image of a golden sun, and next to it was a striking wooden carving.

It was dirty with age and peppered with woodworm holes but the carving was undeniably meant to represent a rat's face.

Pulling the ribbon from her head, Scabmona kicked her way through the paper and honked with laughter.

'Did you ever see such an ugly mug?' she hooted. 'What a daft, dopey kisser!'

Fleabee glared at her impatiently. She was eager to climb the steps and race amongst those happy, irritating mice. Striding through the tattered debris to pull her sister after her, she halted.

The face that had been chiselled and gouged out of the wood was the kindest she had ever seen. The eyes were wide apart and gentle, and the long snout was sandwiched between thick curling whiskers. Two square, peg-like teeth projected from the bottom jaw

above a tightly rolled beard and the mouth was lifted into the most wonderful, benign smile, free from any trace of malice or cruelty.

Scabmona was still laughing but Fleabee moved closer and lifted her claw to touch it.

The iron leaves of the Grille thrashed and coiled feverishly as if trying to prevent her.

'Mouseys must be barmy!' Scabmona snickered, finally getting her mirth under control. 'What a load of rubbish, they deserve to be doofered.'

A sharp gasp escaped Fleabee's lips and she snatched her hand back. The moment she touched the wood a hot, prickling sensation had crackled up her arm and she squeezed her eyes shut as her head began to throb and ache.

Scabmona was too busy sorting through the fallen sticks to notice. Weighing one in her fist she grunted and swung it a few times for practice.

'Should crack a few heads with this,' she said with a wicked grin. 'Knock 'em out and pile the bodies high.'

Fleabee rubbed her eyes then blinked them open. The infernal scarlet light that Jupiter had set there was extinguished – the bloodlust was gone from her forever. She was her usual, tender-hearted self.

The forces that controlled the Grille were quenched and the iron fronds slid back to their positions, becoming solid and immovable once more.

'I know who you are,' she murmured with a faint smile.

Now it was Scabmona's turn to be impatient. 'What you twittering about?' she demanded. 'I've got bloomering to do!'

Warily Fleabee reached out again but this time when she stroked the face, nothing happened.

''Orace Baldmony,' she said softly. 'That's who you're supposed to be, made by some mousey a long time ago, in memory of their friend. Even though you brought death and horror to them, they still made this in memory of you.'

Hearing that reviled name, Scabmona came stamping back and spat in one of the wooden eyes.

'You dirty traitor!' she yelled. 'Filthy snivelling coward. Pulling apart was too good fer you!'

And she began hitting the carving with her stick, until Fleabee dragged her away and wrested the weapon from her grasp.

'You cracked?' Scabmona bawled. 'I want to chew the ears off it and kick them teeth out!'

Ignoring her, Fleabee carefully wiped the spit from the eye. 'I'm sorry for what happened to you,' she said in a sad whisper.

The dappled light that shone through the small window above trembled slightly and, as it played over the wooden image, the shadows beneath the cheeks shifted. It was as if 'Orace had smiled at her.

'You stop here and talk bonkers if you want,' Scabmona snorted in disgust. 'I'm going to split some skulls!'

Seizing another stick, she marched to the bottom step and began clambering up it.

Fleabee was horrified. She could not believe that only moments ago, she too had shared that savagery. The thought of what she had intended to do made her feel sick.

Haring after her sister, she caught hold of Scabmona's foot just as she had scaled the first step and was preparing to tackle the next, and tore her away.

'Hey!' Scabmona screeched. 'Lemme at 'em! I want to take some leftovers home for Alf and Old Klakk! Get off, you mad lousebag!'

'You leave them mouseys alone!' Fleabee commanded, dragging her sister by her hair. 'You'll not eat a single one of them today.'

Scabmona twisted around and bit Fleabee's arm to get free. Then she kicked her and leaped at the step again.

But Fleabee was determined. Once again she wrenched her sister away and frog-marched her back to the Grille.

'Get through there!' she told her in a voice more stern than anything Scabmona had ever heard from her before.

Scabmona hesitated. The desire for fresh mouse was

unbearable within her, yet this angry and resolute Fleabee was something new and unsettling.

'Hate you!' she spat. 'More than I hate him.' And she threw her stick at the carving of 'Orace Baldmony.

Her aim was not good however and the stick went hurtling into the great biscuit-tin lid. There was a vibrating gong-like chime and the disc gave a lurch before rolling across the cellar.

Fleabee and her sister watched it smash into a crate, then spin in a ruinous circle and go clanging to the ground. The noise was tremendous, like a hundred bells tolling some dreadful, deafening alarm. It shook the air and the paper decorations eddied about as if in shock.

The echoes rebounded from wall to wall and box to box – even the paint tins thrummed to the clamour, until Fleabee doubted that they would ever die away.

Eventually, after what seemed an age, the last disturbance tinkled into silence and Fleabee scowled at Scabmona.

'Go,' she ordered.

Scabmona stuck out her tongue, retrieved the throttledoll she had discarded, grabbed the silver and blue mask, then crawled back through the Grille.

'Wait till I tell Old Klakk what you did,' she threatened. 'You'll catch it when we get back. And what's to stop me coming back here whenever I fancy?

Not you, you dozy lump, I'll see to that.'

Grumbling and swearing, Scabmona trudged reluctantly down the shaft, back into the sewers.

Fleabee heaved a great sigh and looked back at the cellar. The relief was almost overwhelming. It was then that she realised the jolly sounds of the mice were no longer to be heard.

'They know there's someone down here,' she muttered to herself. 'They must be terrified.'

As if in answer, a muffled, nervous voice rang out behind the door.

'You can't go in there, Mr Brown! You might get killed!'

'Don't be silly, Oswald,' answered an older but still cautious voice. 'It's probably just that fortune-teller come back again. I'll only take a look.'

Swiftly, Fleabee darted through the Grille but did not go running down the shaft. Instead she pulled herself into the shadows and waited, her gaze fixed on the door in the distance.

A slice of brighter daylight swept into the cellar as the door was heaved open a chink and a small, wary face peered round.

Albert Brown stared in at the wreckage caused by Scabmona, and cleared his throat.

'Hello?' he called a little fearfully. 'Is there anyone down there?'

Fleabee beamed a great smile. He was the first mouse she had ever seen. His face was happily plump, with twinkling eyes, framed by creases set there by much laughter. She liked him immediately. Looking across to where the carving of 'Orace Baldmony stood, she nodded with gratitude.

'Thank you,' she whispered.

Two other mice peeped over Albert Brown's shoulder.

'Can't see anyone, Jacob,' Albert declared.

'A draught then?'

'Must've been. It's blown some of our decorations about the place but it's all quiet and empty now.'

The mice withdrew their heads and pushed the door shut.

A group of frightened neighbours stared at them apprehensively. A tall, albino mouse swaddled in a long green scarf waved his paws in a panic.

'Are you sure, Mr Brown? Are you sure? They might be hiding!'

Albert's eyes sparkled at him. 'Oswald, Oswald,' he

laughed. 'There's nothing to fear down there, trust me. Now, where's young Tom Cockle? Let's have some music. There's no hideous rats down there and never will be neither – I promise.'

Behind the Grille, Fleabee was glad that the mice had not seen her. Noiselessly scurrying down the shaft, she headed for home. But her heart was heavy when she imagined what tales Scabmona would tell their parents.

7
Something Fishy

It took longer for Fleabee to find her way back to the rat domain than she had anticipated. She and Scabmona had been running so blindly in the maze of sewers that she had no idea where she was. It was very late when she finally found herself walking beneath the guttering torches that lit the tunnel of their home.

More by luck than navigation, Scabmona had arrived there a full hour earlier and had told Klakkweena everything. Rancid Alf had not returned since his banishment so Fleabee had only one furious parent to face.

Klakkweena was more than capable of making up for that however. The screams that Fleabee was subjected to were appalling and she was cuffed about the ears until they glowed and her head hurt.

'What are we going to do with you?' her mother raged. 'A whole house of squeakers and you didn't bring back even a small one! I don't know what ails you, child, but you're not natural! This softy sickly nonsense has got to stop. By all that's stinking – I don't know what to do about it if even Jupiter's words can't change you. You're a freak, that's what you are!'

Scabmona bit the nose of her throttledoll with pleasure and enjoyed every minute of this monumental scolding. 'Bash her again,' she insisted. 'Them mouseys sounded plump and squishy!'

Klakkweena was going to do that anyway.

'First thing tomorrow,' she squawked. 'You take me and your dad to that cellar and we bring back as many as we can carry. If we salt 'em they'll keep a bit longer, although I do like it when they hang for a bit and the flies have had a chance to get acquainted.'

'But I wouldn't know how to get back there,' Fleabee wept. 'I really wouldn't, I got lost so many times trying to find my way back here.'

'Don't look at me, Klakk!' Scabmona protested. 'I wouldn't know neither. Real long ways off, that were!'

Klakkweena tore the bristle wig from her head and threw it at them in the worst temper they had ever witnessed. Then she jumped up and down, shrieked for all her lungs were worth, coughed and tore at her straggly hair.

'Is that the foghorn solo of my very own sewer fairy I hear?' a sudden voice called into the rat hole. 'What a pimple-popping serenade to come back to.'

Klakkweena whipped around and gnashed her fangs. Rancid Alf had returned.

'And what do you think you're doing, dragging your worthless hide indoors? Don't you dare put one toe in here or I'll chop it clean off! You're the root of all this! There was never no custard-hearted cowards in my family before – oh no! Get out, you ...'

To her bewilderment, Alf was smiling at her and continued to smile, no matter what dreadful insult she flung at him.

''Ere,' she cried. 'What ails you? Got banged on the head? Why you struck so dumb?'

Rancid Alf flicked his whiskers. 'If Madam would stand aside,' he said in an affected voice, 'your supper awaits.'

'You're a loony,' she told him, backing away slightly.

Alf looked down his snout at her then clicked his claws.

At that signal, Flake and Vinegar Pete came striding in, looking very haughty and superior, carrying a whole piece of battered cod between them.

'M'Lady,' they both said, bowing low and placing the fish on the floor.

Alf clapped his claws and they spun around and

marched in a regimented fashion from the rat hole.

Before Klakkweena could utter any exclamation, Leering Macky entered with his head held very high – bearing nearly an entire packet of peanuts and a great slab of fruitcake.

'Mudum,' he said, dumping them at her feet.

'What's this?' was all she could splutter. 'What's this?'

Rancid Alf winked at Leering Macky as the rat departed, then coughed into his claw.

''Tis the finest high cuisine what we could scrape together,' he declared. 'For the conscrumption and toothly pleasure of the First Lady of the Sewers – the beeyootiful Klakkweena.'

With a heaving chest, the ratwife looked at him and muttered something gruff and unintelligible under her breath.

Rancid Alf cupped his ragged ear. 'What was that, M'Lady?' he asked.

'You're a daft old drunken nose-wipe, Alf,' she said huskily. 'But you're my nose-wipe and that's all I'll say. Don't hang about out there, come on in.'

Alf obeyed.

'Took me an' the lads all day to scavenge this lot,' he said, proudly brushing some tea leaves and ash from the fish. 'Not quite yer actual à la carte, but the bins we found 'em in did have wheels on.'

Scabmona had heard quite enough of this mushy talk and, unable to wait any longer, she snatched a handful of battered cod and shovelled it in her mouth.

Klakkweena and Alf sat close together and tucked in. It was a noisy, messy feast and Klakkweena's rancour was so mollified by the meal that she had no objection to Fleabee joining them.

When they were all as full as they could be and had reached that most dreamed-of state of being completely glutted and there were still some peanuts left, Fleabee and Scabmona staggered to their room. There they lay on the beds, patting their stomachs appreciatively and sucking sultanas and glacé cherries from between their teeth.

With her wigwam-shaped bristle wig wedged back in place, Klakkweena allowed Alf's arm to stray around her shoulders and they stared into the flame of the candle stub that lit their squalid den.

'If we could scoff like that every night,' she sighed. 'I'd have to claw out a wider doorway.'

'Well, tomorrow is Firstblood and there'll be plenty of tasty scraps and morsels fer us then, as well,' said Alf.

Klakkweena's quarrelsome face scrunched up with thought. 'Firstblood,' she repeated, with a dry click of her tongue. 'Our Fleabee's done for, you know. The oath-taking didn't do her no good today. After midnight tomorrow we have to kick her out of here and she's fair game for any roaming rat with a blade.'

'Them's the rules,' Alf shrugged. 'We can't do nowt for her, we tried everything.'

The ratwife nodded.

'Only herself to blame,' she agreed. 'Why does she have to be so pukily pleasant?'

'It'll serve her right.'

'Well I, for one, won't be sorry to have her gone.'

There was a pause as they considered this. Having been brought up under Jupiter's harsh regime, neither of them could admit to what they really felt.

Rancid Alf's ears drooped and turned pale. He coughed to clear the lump in his throat and quickly changed the subject.

'So is Alf forgiven for not bringing the duck home?' he asked. 'Weren't this a whole lot better? Did Madam find it to her liking?'

111

Klakkweena made no answer – she was staring absently into the candle flame.

Alf nudged her but there was no response.

He nudged her again.

Nothing.

Alf pinched her.

Klakkweena clouted him across the snout.

'I should've thought of it before!' she cried excitedly. 'If His High and Scary Mightiness can't turn our Fleabee rotten, then there's always...'

Her voice dropped to a whisper. 'There's always them what were here before Him.'

Rubbing his sore snout, Alf began to protest. 'Now you listen 'ere,' he hissed. 'That's proper dangerous, that is! You know that's forbid more than owt else. Why, you can't even say their names without it getting reported and scribbled down in Wormy Ned's plaguey book. Him and Morgan will have you, they will.'

'They won't know about it,' Klakkweena swore. 'It's a cure we need, but not from no faker down here. You calling me Madam back then put me in mind of it. She'll be close by. She's not missed a Firstblood in years. Morgan mightn't be able to stick the sight of her but he leaves her alone.'

'What?' Alf exclaimed. 'Her! She's barmier than a red hot bucket of gouty hedgehogs.'

Klakkweena's mind was made up. 'She's our

Fleabee's best chance,' she said, lurching to her feet. 'I'm going to take her there right now.'

'Well I'm having nowt to do with this,' he said firmly. 'If you get caught goin' up top, you're on your own.'

'You just keep Scabmona here, I don't want her trailing us.'

Into their daughters' sleeping chamber the ratwife carefully stepped, hoping not to wake Scabmona. Placing a claw over Fleabee's mouth, she shook her and the ratgirl struggled awake.

'Hush,' Klakkweena breathed. 'Get up and come with me.'

'Where you two going?' Scabmona demanded in a loud, vexed voice, as she sprang up in her bed like a malignant jack-in-the-box.

Klakkweena groaned. 'Get back to sleep,' she told her.

'Won't! I want to know where you're going.'

'On a little spree, that's all.'

'What you taking that lumpy pudding for, then? She's no use to no one.'

'Keep your snout out of this or I'll do to you what I used to do to my throttledoll.'

Scabmona folded her arms and glowered at the pair of them.

Klakkweena led a drowsy Fleabee from the rat hole

and took the last of the peanuts with her, much to Alf's dismay.

'Don't let no one see you,' he warned, as they left.

'Where we going?' Fleabee asked, wiping the sleep from her eyes. 'I told you I don't know how to find that cellar again.'

Her mother bade her to be quiet. As they made their way along the ledge, many curious faces poked out of nearby holes and threw suspicious, nosey glances after them.

'Off for a stroll, are we?' sniggered a very fat ratwife whose hair was matted and stuck with twigs.

'Evenin', Hagnakker.' Klakkweena greeted her with a fixed, unpleasant grin. 'Just taking our Fleabee off for an overdue dunking in the mud pits. Might be the last chance I get.'

Hagnakker approved whole-heartedly. 'You be certain the abnormal little weirdo don't enjoy it!' she advised. 'Gives me the creeps, that one does.'

Klakkweena bit her tongue and walked past. Now was not the time to trade insults. Hagnakker had other ideas.

'Jam and vinegar,' she said. 'That's what you've got for daughters. There's this hoity-toity, slime wouldn't melt, good-for-the-sake-of-it princess and then there's that other one. Belongs on a chain, that rabid Scabmona does. What does she think she is? A mad mongrel, that's what my Fletch calls her. Go too far one day, she will.'

This was too much and Klakkweena wheeled about.

'Oh, how is your spotty-nosed Fletch?' she inquired, the grin now nailed to her face.

Hagnakker eyed her doubtfully. 'What's it to you?' she demanded.

'Only that he didn't look too well before, when he was round at ours,' Klakkweena lied through her fangs.

'He weren't at yours. He were gamblin' with his cronies.'

'Oh, is that what he said?'

'He said it 'cos that's what he were doin'.'

Klakkweena shrugged. 'Always did bolt his grub down, didn't he?'

Hagnakker's fat face twitched. 'What's this?' she snapped.

'You did hear about the feast my Alf brought in tonight? Oh – it were so huge we couldn't never guzzle it all, so your Fletch bailed us out, so to speak.'

A thundercloud passed over her neighbour's face. 'That Macky did say summat before,' she muttered, through tight lips. 'And you're telling me that my Fletch helped you wolf it down and didn't bring one crumb of batter back to me?'

Klakkweena looked shocked. 'But I gave him a claw full of cod and three big peanuts specially for you. I wouldn't see you deprived.'

'Well he brung nowt back here!' came the fuming retort.

Klakkweena tutted. 'I did think it funny, how he went off in the direction of Boglina's hole instead of here,' she said with arched brows.

By then she was speaking to empty air. Hagnakker had stormed back into her own den and her screeches and the innocent wails of her mate rang throughout the tunnel.

Satisfied at not only successfully wiping the smug smirk off her neighbour's flabby face for the time being, but also providing herself and Fleabee with a wonderful diversion, Klakkweena took her daughter's arm once more and continued on their way.

Once the light of the torches was far behind them, Klakkweena hastened their pace.

'Where are we going?' Fleabee asked again. 'You're not really going to throw me in the muds, are you?'

Her mother shook her head. 'I ought to,' she said. 'The amount of trouble you cause.'

'Where, then?'

Klakkweena stopped for a moment and quickly looked about them. 'You're a strange one, my girl,' she declared. 'I never could fathom what whirrs in your skull and I gave up trying a long time ago. So curse me if I know why I'm taking this last bother now, but if anyone finds out, then we'll both be fer it!'

'I won't tell anyone,' Fleabee promised. 'Trust me.'

'There you go again!' Klakkweena cried. 'What other rat would say that and mean it? None! Even your sister would peach on me and I wouldn't blame her – it's expected, you see. You, you're different and as unlike the rest as it's possible to be. When you saved Alf from that duck, that's a thing I wouldn't do. Each fer themselves, it says in Wormy Ned's book of rules, but none of that ever sunk in up there, did it?'

Fleabee lowered her eyes. 'I'm not a true rat of Deptford,' she confessed unhappily. 'I can't do what Him in that portal wants, I really can't, Mother.'

'I know,' Klakkweena groaned. 'You an' me might live underground and look like mucky potatoes, but you're no spud – you keep sproutin' out flippin' flowers.' She looked at her daughter sharply. 'Well, maybe I've an idea why.'

'How do you mean?'

Her mother glanced around them again and, finding that place suddenly full of shadows where any number of ears might be listening, she took the ratgirl's claw and hurried through a passageway before saying another word.

'What I tell you now,' she resumed, 'is worth my skin, so remember that.'

Fleabee nodded, intrigued by this sudden furtive secrecy.

'Jupiter weren't always here,' Klakkweena whispered.

'Oh yes, He's ruled us for hundreds of years but before Him … there were others.'

'Others?'

'Not so loud, not so loud. He don't let them be mentioned. The last who did that was Old Manky, you wasn't born then, that's going back to when I was a ratling. Always had a reputation for being a bit of a witch, did Old Manky. Folk'd go to her for ointments and potions she'd brewed herself. Only small stuff, nothing to worry the bosses, but they watched her close. Then one day she blundered by claiming her gifts came from the Three, and that was enough to have her chucked past the candles – into Jupiter's own darkness. She were never seen again: no one who goes in there comes out alive.'

Fleabee frowned. 'The Three what?' she asked.

Her mother jumped nervously and hushed her again. Hurrying under an archway and running along a pipe, she waited several minutes before answering.

'The Three true Gods of the rats!' she eventually declared in a reverential breath, tracing a circle upon her forehead. 'The Raith Sidhe.'

'Never heard of them.'

Klakkweena grunted in exasperation and dragged her further into another tunnel.

'Course you ain't – you're not meant to. They're s'posed to be forgotten. But some of us remember, some of us know and, this night, so will you. Now, the way up's not far.'

Fleabee choked with delight. 'We're going outside?' she marvelled. 'To the upper world?'

'Yes,' her mother answered, with a shudder. 'There's someone I wants you to meet.'

'Who?'

She had to wait for the answer. They had reached an iron railing that projected vertically from the sewer wall. It reared high over their heads, disappearing up into the blackness of a drain that opened above them like a vast chimney.

'This isn't the way Flake brought us,' Fleabee said.

Her mother laughed. 'There's more than one way out,' she said. 'We all think we got our own hidden routes and nobody else knows 'em. But I'll wager Jupiter does. He's lived and lurked down here too long not to have had His spies sniff every path. Yes, He knows but maybe He can't watch everything at

119

once. Maybe if the luck is with us we'll sneak out without Him knowing.'

The railing was the rusted remains of an old ladder but it was enough for a rat to clamber up and, proving herself more nimble than Fleabee had ever suspected, Klakkweena jumped up and began to climb. Fleabee followed her, her mind overflowing with questions.

Higher and higher they went and Fleabee's claws ached. Her mother's breaths turned to wheezes and she could hear her mumbling curses to herself.

Then at last it was over. The railing ended abruptly and Klakkweena swung herself on to a stone ledge that jutted from the wall. There she puffed and panted, holding her chest as she slumped wearily against the bricks.

'Not ... done that for a long time,' she coughed. 'Used to be able to swarm up that in a gnat's blink, I did. A gutful of fish and cake and peanuts don't lighten the load, neither.'

Fleabee was soon standing beside her and looking upwards. A choked, snarled ceiling of dried grass and bramble that had crept down from the outside world and withered in the dark, hung over their heads. It smelt of must and sweet decay and the ratgirl's heart beat a little faster. She could sense the outside world was very close.

'Must hurry,' Klakkweena said, reaching up with

her claws to drag the wild tangled thatch away and send big clumps of it floating down to the sewers below. 'Don't want to be up top any longer than I need to.'

In moments it was done. A draught of clean cold air came flooding from above and the familiar orange light of a street lamp poured in.

Klakkweena wasted no time. She hauled herself out through the hole she had made and hissed at Fleabee to follow.

The ratgirl was already scrambling upwards and before the words were out of Klakkweena's mouth, she was standing at her side.

Fleabee took great savouring breaths of the March night and looked about her, enthralled.

They had emerged in a deserted alleyway, overgrown with monstrous thickets of buddleia and bramble that had broken through the flagstones of the pavement. A high wooden fence towered up on the right-hand side and a burned-out warehouse rose on the left. It reeked of wet charcoal and cinders. Fleabee did not like the look of it.

She shifted her gaze upward and smiled at the sky. The night was clear and every star was blazing, but she was not permitted to admire it for long.

'Stop gawking!' Klakkweena scolded impatiently. 'This way, this way.'

Into the forest of thorns and twigs her mother darted, hacking a path with her claws to the bottom of the fence, searching for a way through.

'Here it is,' she said at length. 'In here!'

One of the planks had rotted away and she jumped through the gap, calling for Fleabee to do the same.

Fleabee hesitated. She was stroking the prickly bramble leaves. She had never understood where leaves came from. Sometimes they floated by on the sewer water but she never dreamed that they actually grew on things like this.

A gruff bark from her mother snatched her attention back to the gap in the fence. Quickly she dropped down and followed.

Beyond lay a new and different country. It was a strange and bleak landscape of rusted metal. Huge hills of great, broken shapes spread out as far as she could see. They were piled as high as buildings, but Fleabee could not begin to guess what they were. They looked like the empty crushed shells of gigantic snails and she peered at them warily. They were blank and dark.

Silence covered all. A bright moon, which had been obscured behind the fence, shone milky and round in the heavens. It cast wells of shadow under every bump and ridge, creating horrible, unfriendly forms and leering faces. Fleabee thought threatening figures were all around her. The reflected moonlight glinted and winked in shards of glass and slivers of mirror, suggesting hungry, watchful eyes to Fleabee's young imagination.

She gave the air a cautious sniff. If there were any monsters lurking nearby, surely she would be able to tell? The ratgirl sighed in relief. Her nostrils sensed only a sharp metallic tang and the pungency of perishing rubber.

Avalanches of worn tyres had slid into the canyons that lay between the heaps of scrap metal. It would have been a perfect playground for Scabmona but it held no interest for Fleabee. Once she was certain there was no immediate danger, she returned her attention to the sky.

'What is that?' she asked, pointing to the moon. 'It's so beautiful.'

A dark shape flitted high above, cutting across the celestial white disc and Fleabee watched it in fascination.

'A bird!' she called out.

Klakkweena laughed at her. 'That's a bat – you daft dollop!' she said, hopping on to the nearest tyre and setting off through the rusted city. 'Don't you have nowt to do with the likes of them.'

'A bat,' her daughter murmured. 'What a place this is up here. So many new things all around.'

'If you dawdle you'll be lost in here,' Klakkweena

warned, hop-scotching her way forward. 'I know only one road through this and won't go hunting for you if you stray.'

Fleabee did her best to keep up. 'But where are we going?' she pleaded. 'You still haven't told me who it is you're taking me to see.'

Her mother halted and turned an almost fearful face to her.

'We're going to the ratwitch,' she said darkly.

8

In the Vale of Metal

Fleabee stumbled and almost slithered down into the centre of the tyre.

'The ratwitch?' she cried. 'Who's that?'

Klakkweena resumed the journey.

'She's the last of her kind,' she said. 'When she's gone there won't be any like her. Not round here, leastways. There ain't no one like Madame Akkikuyu.'

Fleabee looked disappointed. 'Do you mean that fortune-teller who visits our tunnels from time to time? She's just bonkers, everyone knows that.'

Her mother leaped back and put a claw to her lips. 'Hush!' she whispered. 'It's not far now, don't you go saying things about what you know nowt of. Akkikuyu knows more than fake fortunes to please the likes of

Boglina. When Akkikuyu's down in Jupiter's realm, she has to pretend. She has to scrape and nod like the rest of us, but she knows plenty more than she cracks on. Don't you doubt that, my girl.'

Fleabee did doubt it. Every ratling knew Madame Akkikuyu by sight and although they enjoyed her mad, eccentric ways, no one, not even Winjeela, could possibly be afraid of her. With a sinking heart, she began to think that this journey was a waste of time and would not help her.

Further into that cluttered, jumbled land they went, until at last Klakkweena crossed over to the lower slope of one of the huge metal hills and gave what looked like a black rubber ball a brutal kick.

A battered trumpet-shaped brass tube stuck out of one end and immediately a loud honk blared out of it. Fleabee jumped back in surprise. Her mother kicked the bulbous thing again and then stamped on it.

Two more fierce throaty blasts issued from the strange instrument, then Klakkweena stood back, straightened her bristle wig and waited.

'What did you do that for?' Fleabee asked.

Klakkweena pulled her ragged garments about her. 'Got to announce ourselves,' she replied. 'Got to let Akkikuyu know we're here and on our way to see her.'

'Not like you to bother about such things.'

Her mother grimaced. 'This ain't like paying a call

on Hagnakker or any of them other drabs down our tunnel,' she muttered, hastily drawing a circle on her forehead once more. 'It don't pay to go upsetting Akkikuyu, and only a feeble-witted fool would try – I don't want no curse put on my ears.'

Fleabee had never realised that her no-nonsense, poison-tongued mother could be so superstitious. She wanted to ask more questions but suddenly a loud yell rang over the scrap yard and, from nowhere, two ribbons of flame came bouncing over the expanse of tyres.

'Ho-A!' cried a voice.

'Eee-Yoo!' roared another.

Klakkweena uttered a frightened squawk and Fleabee pressed close to her.

'Fire devils!' the ratwife shrieked. 'She must be angry with us!'

Swiftly the fiery streaks hurtled forward, leaping and rushing at tremendous speed. Then, abruptly, they were upon them.

The rats covered their faces, expecting their whiskers to be scorched right off. Moments crept by but nothing happened and they opened their eyes timidly.

Standing before them were two extremely odd-looking but identical creatures. They looked like small rats but their tails were hairy and their fur was the colour of sand. Flowing, scarlet scarves were tied about their middles and they wore spangled black waistcoats. They had the longest legs and the biggest feet that Fleabee had ever seen. Large, inquisitive eyes bulged in their heads, glittering under the torches that they each held aloft.

Klakkweena returned their curious stares with a hostile one of her own and pursed her lips irritably. Seeing that she was considerably taller than them, she pulled herself together and folded her arms.

"Ere!' she demanded. 'Who are you? What you doing jumpin' about like over-sized fleas and pouncin' on folk?'

The strangers looked at one another and began chattering in a language that neither Fleabee nor her mother could understand. Then they both nodded simultaneously and with a 'Whoop!' they bounded away, their torches painting a bright trail behind them.

Into the distance streaked the streams of light and the rats were left blinking in the moonlight.

'What … what were they?' Fleabee stammered in surprise.

Klakkweena shook her head. 'Never seen the likes of them before. Foreigners, whatever, all that bouncin' around would make them real tricky to catch, never mind trying to peel them. Good thing for them I'm still full of Alf's fish supper or I'd try and have a go.'

Fleebee opened her mouth to say something but the fiery torches were zooming back again and with a whoosh of flame and a triumphant, 'Hoo-La-Ooop!' the creatures landed in front of them once more. This time they were not alone.

A fluffy, wide-faced, honey-coloured hamster with sleepy eyes was held suspended between them. The newcomer was wrapped in a dark blue cloak that almost, but not quite, hid his tiny pink feet, which were dangling in mid-air.

After looking long and hard at the two rats, he said something in their weird language to the creatures supporting him and they promptly set him down with a flourish and a bow.

'You wish to see the Great and Cosmic Akkikuyu?' he addressed Klakkweena in a theatrical tone.

The ratwife was taken aback by the question, but quickly collected her base wits and glared at him.

'Who wants to know?' she growled.

To Klakkweena and Fleabee's astonishment, the hamster opened his mouth wide, reached in and brought out from one of the pouches in his cheeks a roll of paper, which he held under the torchlight and consulted closely.

'You don't look like an arthritic mole,' he said at length. 'Either of you – and he's the only one listed here for tonight. You don't appear to have made an appointment. No rats are listed here I'm afraid, my dear.'

'Appointment?' the ratwife snapped. 'Since when do we need one of them to consult with her?'

The hamster rolled up the paper and deposited it back in his cheek before answering. 'Since we fell in with her. We don't let any scraggy old nobody visit unless they make an appointment first of all. Got to do things properly, you know. I don't like this hotchpotch approach. Too many amateurs in the world as it is.'

'And who in the name of the blazing pits are you?'

'We are travelling artistes,' the hamster replied with a professional smile and an ebullient wave of his short arms. 'My colleagues, Vasili and Tilik are The Flying Mongolians, a wonderfully acrobatic act, as you no doubt have gathered. They really are superb but they don't speak a word of English except "yes" and "no" and "chocolate finger".'

At the mention of their names, his two friends bowed once more and said, in unison and with thick accents, 'Yes, yes – chocolate finger!'

Fleabee laughed, but her mother sniffed disagreeably. 'What sort of freaks are they, then?' she asked. 'And what are you? Look like a flattened mouse to me, you do.'

'Nuff is my name,' said the hamster, disregarding her rudeness as though he were used to such vulgar observations. 'Or rather, that is the one I was saddled with in my former life as a captive. I won't go into that now, don't press me, don't probe. Those are dark days of running endlessly round in a wheel without ever getting anywhere and having to climb into a velour settee to escape those huge petting hands – eurgh! Oh, the indignity of it all.'

He shuddered at the memory, then composed himself and turned a smiling face upon Fleabee. 'Still, Nuff is a pleasant enough name. I have far too many other important tasks that wrestle for my attention to try and think of a new one.'

'But what are you?' Klakkweena persisted and she gave the cloak a suspicious glance. 'You got a tail under there or was it cut off?'

Nuff coughed defensively. 'I have a tail,' he declared. 'It might not be as long as yours, but it serves me well enough. Size isn't everything, you know. I'm a hamster, not a rat.'

'Hamster?' Klakkweena repeated, rolling the word round her mouth as though sampling a new and unexpected morsel. 'Never heard of it. Unless you're something to do with bacon?'

'And my two fine colleagues,' Nuff continued, ignoring her again, 'are fellow escapees from that dark history of mine. Mine was the mastermind behind our victorious getaway, by the way. They're gerbils you know, brothers, and rather splendid with it. I've managed to pick up the language quite well, but they're more than a tad slow at doing the same.'

Tilik and Vasili grinned and struck heroic poses.

'Yes, yes!' they declared.

'We're rehearsing,' Nuff explained. 'We've been wintering here ever since breaking free and have been putting the act together. It's a slow process and fraught with tantrums and differences of artistic interpretation. They are very hot-tempered you know, but I'm the one with the vision and know what works best.'

Klakkweena was growing impatient. 'Where is Akkikuyu?' she demanded. 'We don't have long.'

'I'm trying to organise a little tour,' the hamster said blithely, directing his chatter at Fleabee. 'Out in the provinces to begin with, before bringing it back to the city. It's almost ready but I still feel we're lacking a certain something.'

He grasped Fleabee's claw and cried, 'Oh, would you watch and be our first audience? Public reaction is so vital. That would be extremely beneficial, it really would!'

'I'd love to!' the ratgirl exclaimed and before her mother could raise an objection, Nuff was giving instructions to the gerbils, and Tilik bounded away.

The hamster scurried over to a clear space on the ground and called back to Fleabee.

'You have to imagine this is a stage with lanterns twinkling all around. And maybe there'll be a curtain, or a painted cloth at the back here. Still – I suppose we'll be playing in all sorts of al fresco venues.'

At that, Tilik came leaping back, carrying a bulky bag and a large bottle-top filled with a clear liquid.

Nuff called out a few more instructions and the gerbils dived into the background, hopping up into the pile of forsaken machinery behind him, until they stood at the very summit, holding their torches high.

'Ladies and gentlemice!' Nuff began in a loud,

practised voice. 'Ladies and gentlerats,' he hastily corrected himself.

'For your delectation and amazement, from the far reaches of Outer Mongolia, we bring you...oh, wait a moment.'

Hurrying over to the bag, he rummaged inside it with his back to his audience, then came scuttling back to the same spot.

'From the far reaches of Outer Mongolia,' he resumed, 'we bring you an act of such daring, such élan – that no one would believe it. We ask you to watch and be astounded and leave this place, believing in champions once more! We give you the one and only – The Flying Mongolians!'

With that a duet of whoops and cries rang out as the gerbils leaped from their lofty perches and plummeted downwards.

Fleabee squealed and threw her claws over her eyes, while Klakkweena cackled and licked her lips.

Long before they hit the floor however, Tilik and Vasili landed on projecting spurs of metal and were catapulted back up, spinning through the air, brandishing the torches – carving out bright patterns in the dark with the flames. Up and down they bounced, sometimes exchanging places, sometimes snatching a torch from the other and juggling two of them in the air.

On the ground, Nuff was also watching, nodding and making mental notes of all that they did and wincing when they missed a signal that only they and he would know.

It was a wonderful display and Fleabee was enchanted, but there was still more to come.

Into the air Nuff threw two more unlit torches and, as the gerbils swooped, they snatched them and lit them so the fiery show became even brighter.

Down they sprang, leaping in a close circle around the hamster, whirling about him faster and faster until he seemed enveloped by a pillar of fire. Then, with a jubilant yell, they jumped back and up into the towers of metal again.

Nuff took another pair of unlit torches from the bag but this time he merely held them aloft and when the acrobats bounded across, they struck them with the others and they erupted in flame.

'What's he going to do with them?' Fleabee breathed.

Klakkweena pretended she wasn't interested and looked at her claws but she stole secret glances upwards when she thought her daughter wasn't looking, which was practically all the time.

Then Nuff hurled the blazing torches upwards. The gerbils caught them smartly.

'Now they have three!' Fleabee spluttered in disbelief. 'Oh don't drop one or burn your paws!'

The glare from the display was almost blinding. Juggling three torches each, Tilik and Vasili created such fabulous designs with skeins of pure flame that the ratgirl's heart leaped to see them.

Shapes of leaves and birds would instantly appear, only to become something new and equally incredible. A large mousebrass glimmered there for a moment, then an acorn, then a wriggling worm. A sickle moon, a bat, a great glowing spider shone out. Then a leering rat's skull, a flower and then suddenly a huge tree with drooping branches burned into being.

Fleabee did not recognise many of the shapes but she cheered all the same and even Klakkweena had to bite her lips to prevent herself from joining in.

The gerbils landed either side of Nuff, but the act was not over. They started throwing the torches over his head and then Tilik took charge of all six torches and kept them soaring.

Vasili lay on his back, stuck his feet in the air and with a dexterous leap, his brother jumped on top of them. There followed an incredible display of balance and timing.

Vasili's legs kicked out. Tilik zoomed upwards. All the torches were blazing and twirling. Tilik performed a somersault. Nuff ran forward, took a swig at the bottle-lid. Vasili bounded to his feet again and jumped clear. Tilik landed lightly a short distance away. Nuff sprang between them. One by one the torches came falling down, wedged themselves into the ground, flames uppermost, forming a perfect ring around the hamster, who threw back his head and spat a jet of brilliant flame high into the night.

For several seconds the beacon blasted a pinnacle of light far above the scrap yard, pointing a searing sword of fire at the moon. The rats felt a wall of heat beating upon them and Klakkweena clasped her jowls in order to stop her jaw falling wide open.

The gerbils threw open their arms and shouted, 'Yes! Yes!'

Then it was over.

The huge flame was extinguished and, after daintily wiping his mouth on a handkerchief, Nuff blew out all but two of the surrounding torches.

Dabbing at his brow, the hamster shuffled forward, huffing and puffing a little.

'Such a terrible taste,' he commented, giving his tongue an airing. 'I don't think I'll ever get accustomed to it. Well, my dears – what did you think?'

Fleabee hardly knew where to begin. 'It was the most marvellous thing I ever saw,' she enthused. 'Wasn't it, Mother?'

Klakkweena shrugged, determined not to betray herself. 'Was all right I s'pose,' she said dryly.

Nuff twitched his nose at her then hurried back to

the gerbils, who were still locked in their triumphant poses. He chattered to them quickly and they nodded, throwing the rats eager glances.

'I told them you both adored it and were gushing with praise,' the hamster said when he returned. 'Of course, what I realise now is that it needs some music – a fanfare or two. I don't suppose either of you is proficient on the bark drum or whisker fiddle? Do you have a reed pipe about your persons? Hmm … perhaps not.'

'Folk will come from all over to see that,' Fleabee sighed. 'With or without music.'

Nuff chortled. 'You can visit us whenever you want to,' he said. 'I'm so pleased you liked it. Are you sure it didn't drag in the middle?'

'I thought it did,' grumbled Klakkweena. 'And at the beginning and at the end.'

'Not at all,' Fleabee reassured him.

'Bless you for that,' he said. 'We'll find out soon enough, we move out of here in a week's time to start the tour. We're very thrilled, we really are. A few more rehearsals and I think we'll have it nailed.'

He ran over to the gerbils again and began gesticulating upwards, explaining the intricacies of certain moves that he was not entirely happy with and seemed to forget that the rats were even there.

'Hoy – Bacon roll!' Klakkweena barked at him.

Nuff looked around. 'Oh forgive me,' he chuckled. 'I do get carried away. Now, what was it you wanted?'

'Akkikuyu!' came the terse reply.

'Oh yes of course. Well as you've been so kind as to sit through our little performance and as that mole is showing no signs of turning up, I'll lead you to her.'

'Don't call me kind,' Klakkweena warned him.

Nuff twirled his paws at the gerbils and Tilik and Vasili grabbed the two burning torches and led the way.

Over the tyres they marched. The brothers jabbered to one another about the act, with Nuff occasionally interjecting with firm refusals at some outlandish suggestion or addition to their routines.

'You have to be very strict as a manager, you know,' he confided in Fleabee. 'They want three changes of costume but who'll end up carrying it all, I ask myself? I had to deny them hats straight off. What a ridiculous notion! Had to stamp my foot very hard about that.'

They reached the far corner from where the gerbils had originally appeared and there, a little distance away, was a ramshackle, flimsy-looking tent that leaned to one side.

Propped up against a great broken engine, it nestled between the shelter of two large, shiny black boxes. It was an incongruous sight. The faded, tattered covering was flapping lazily in the breeze but there was no light within. In front of the entrance the ground was strewn with cubes of broken glass, overturned pots, rummaged-through bundles and over-stuffed bags.

Klakkweena eyed the messy jumble appreciatively. That was how a rat should live, in a glorious disorder of discarded wreckage.

'Wee-Oo!' Tilik and Vasili cried out together and in three bounds they were standing outside the tent, planting their torches in the ground.

'Madame!' Nuff called. 'Madame. You have visitors.'

There was a grunt and a hiss within the tent.

The gerbils stooped to pick up a length of copper wire each and leaped on to the large black boxes.

'Who out there?' came a bad-tempered voice. 'What they want?'

'They are two of your kind,' the hamster answered. 'They have come to seek you out and petition the glorious kingdoms beyond this mortal veil.'

'Tell them go – Akkikuyu busy. She communing with the dark spirits and the infinites.'

'Via a bottle, I imagine,' Nuff murmured under his breath, but he turned to Fleabee and her mother and said apologetically, 'I'm terribly sorry. I do believe she's indisposed.'

'No she ain't,' Klakkweena snapped back. 'She's in that tent!'

The hamster coughed into his paw. 'She can't see you tonight,' he explained. 'Maybe tomorrow or the day after. I'll make a special appointment for you.'

'We don't have time fer that,' the ratwife shrieked. 'It's now or not at all and we ain't going till we see her.'

Nuff scrutinised her resolute face and knew there was no budging her. 'If you would be so accommodating as to wait here, I'll see what can be done,' he said. 'I might be able to persuade Her Great Mystickness to sally forth.'

Lifting the skirts of his cloak he hurried to the tent and popped his head inside.

There was a heated and hasty exchange and the hamster withdrew his head.

'What have you got?' he asked Klakkweena. 'She's not going to … er … disturb her conference with the spirits for nothing.'

Klakkweena held up the remaining peanuts in the bag.

Nuff bowed and muttered something into the tent out of the side of his mouth.

'From the baking, distant desert sands,' he proclaimed, rearing himself up to his full but very short height. 'From the hot, scorched lands of magic, mystery and secret devotions, I give you the one, the only, Madame Akkikuyu – Moroccan Mistress of the Occult and all its supernatural forces!'

Stepping away from the tent, he began applauding.

Upon the boxes, Tilik and Vasili dragged the wires across metal points and a shower of electric sparks suddenly exploded into the air, showering down a

142

glittering rain of golden stars that was reflected in the broken glass on the ground.

Fleabee marvelled. It looked potently magical and her opinion of the fortune-teller rocketed.

Lit by this crackling downpour, Madame Akkikuyu emerged slowly from the tent.

She was a powerfully-built black rat, with a long bone that she used to stir her noxious brews thrust into her wild hair, and a spotted red shawl wrapped around her shoulders. Many pendants and talismans swung from her neck and upon her right ear was a crude tattoo of a grinning face.

'I am Akkikuyu!' she declared grandly. 'I divine the future – I am Akkikuyu!'

The hamster viewed her critically. He had tried to show her how to make an impressive entrance but she was still extremely wooden about it. He gestured to Tilik and Vasili and they stopped what they were doing. The sparks ceased and Akkikuyu looked at the rats who had come to see her.

'Akkikuyu know you,' she said to Klakkweena. 'Sewer folk! Rats of Him who rules beneath.'

Alarmed at hearing this, Nuff edged away from them. Even he had heard of the ferocity of Jupiter's subjects and a frightened expression twitched on to his face.

'Tilik, Vasili!' he called, beckoning to them hurriedly

as he made his excuses to the rats. 'We must go and rehearse until they're perfect. And I still have my impromptu recitations to practise. Goodbye.'

Fleabee waved and he fluttered a flustered paw in her direction. Then the gerbils were at his side and, at a command from him in their language, they grabbed hold of his elbows and sprang away.

'Chocolate finger!' they shouted as they disappeared into the moonlit distance. 'Yes – yes?'

And then they were gone.

'What you want of Akkikuyu?' the black rat demanded in a sudden voice that jolted back Fleabee's attention. 'Potions? Card reading? Charms to ward off sickness or to cause it? Amulets for love maybe? Come, approach – sit, sit, Akkikuyu not bite – she scry your destinies.'

Klakkweena led a wary Fleabee closer. They sat on two overturned pots and the black rat settled herself down.

'It's not a fortune we need telling,' Klakkweena began. 'Not one of your bogus ones anyways, you don't have to pretend all that with me. I want you to have a good long look at my daughter here, and tell me what you see. What's in store for her, that's what we need to know.'

Madame Akkikuyu turned her great dark eyes upon Fleabee. Holding the ratgirl's chin, she pushed her face left, then right, examined her palms and ears then leaned back and smiled faintly.

'Pretty ratlet,' she croaked. 'You have fine daughter, you lucky. What wrong?'

Fleabee smiled back at her. She liked the fortune-teller.

'It's Firstblood tomorrow,' Klakkweena explained.

'Akkikuyu know. Akkikuyu be there. She enjoy rat feast.'

'Don't we all. But this 'ere pain in the whiskers ain't blue-murdered no one yet.'

'Ah,' said the black rat with a twinkle in her eye for Fleabee. 'Busy night she have, then.'

'That's the very point of it!' Klakkweena went on. 'She won't never blue-murder no one. She's no true rat, leastways not one of … His! Even the oath didn't work on her.'

Madame Akkikuyu regarded Fleabee with surprise. 'Magic oath not take? Jupiter's spells not chain you and set heat in your blood? Most interesting, ratlet. Akkikuyu wonder why.'

'I don't know,' Fleabee answered. 'I don't want to harm anything, that's all.'

Klakkweena held her face in her claws. 'Listen to her!' she wailed. 'The awful shame of it! Me, the daughter of Black Ratchet, lumbered with a Milkmite, Sickweed runt.'

Madame Akkikuyu reached into one of her bulging bags and brought out a globe of glass with a swirl of colour in its centre.

'Akkikuyu look in crystal,' she said solemnly. 'It will tell all.'

'What I don't get,' Klakkweena continued to whine, 'is that she weren't born under the sign of the Mouse, she were slap-bang in the House of Mabb.'

Fleabee stared at her mother. 'What are you talking about?' she asked in confusion.

Not taking her eyes from the globe, Madame Akkikuyu cackled. 'Ha!' she said. 'The Rat Zodiac, it still forbid in sewer land?'

Klakkweena nodded sulkily.

'I don't understand,' her daughter muttered. 'I've never heard of that.'

Akkikuyu moved her claws over the crystal. 'Many things kept hid behind clamped teeth down in tunnels of the living God,' she said. 'Zodiac very old, old as ancient tales and more. Times of year are special, when you born determine who you be. Akkikuyu born in the sign of the Vagabond and she's tramped the world ever since.'

'Have you really been around the world?' Fleabee asked. 'What's it like?'

Madame Akkikuyu sucked her teeth as she considered. 'Full of pain, ratlet,' she eventually replied. 'Lost hopes never found, lost loves buried in ditches deep and yearning wishes destroyed. The paths are paved with broke hearts and broke heads. Peril and

146

fear lurk under stones and hate hides in trees. World is bad place.'

'I was the sign of Discord,' Klakkweena butted in with a proud toss of the head. 'A common Brawler, same as my dad.'

'And what of ratlet?' sang Akkikuyu. 'I look – I see.'

The fortune-teller stared deeper into the crystal.

The only thing she saw was a distorted, swollen reflection of her own snout and the usual misting over as she breathed too heavily down her nostrils. She professed to own supernatural powers and had always longed and yearned for them but had never been blessed with such fabulous gifts.

She was, however, capable of making shrewd and lucky guesses from time to time.

'Ratlet came crying under the sign of the Ratwitch,' she declared and Klakkweena gasped in agreement.

'That she did! That's why I brought her here to you.'

Madame Akkikuyu mumbled some strange words under her breath then lifted her eyes and shook her head.

'This ratlet not for Jupiter,' she declared. 'Her heart never follow Lord of the Sewers, her own path she must seek, who know what will pave it? Mabb will guide her, Mabb will show the way.'

Klakkweena whistled softly through her teeth. 'Our Fleabee, chosen by Mabb?'

'Who is this Mabb?' Fleabee asked, looking from one to the other.

'Ratlet not know of the Three?' Madame Akkikuyu tutted.

'You know we can't speak of them down there,' Klakkweena answered. 'Morgan would throw me to Jupiter if he even knew I was here talking about them.'

The fortune-teller returned the crystal to her bag then brought out a grubby-looking pack of cards and began searching through them.

'Long time ago,' she said in a grave voice to Fleabee, 'there were the Three. Ancient gods of the ratfolk and other wild things.'

'The Raith Sidhe,' Klakkweena nudged her daughter.

'Most terrible is Lord Hobb,' Akkikuyu declared, removing a card and giving it to the girl. 'Him very feared, a demon in rat shape.'

Fleabee stared at the card in her claws. A frightful picture was painted on it of a hideous, horned rat enveloped by infernal flame.

'It's horrible,' she whispered.

'Hobb very scaresome,' Akkikuyu agreed. 'Him not nice – oh no.'

She took another card from the pack and passed it over. This depicted a headless, dancing figure.

'Bauchan,' said Akkikuyu. 'The artful one – Old Crafty.'

Fleabee peered at it. 'Why doesn't he have a head?'

''Cos he can wear whatever head he likes,' her mother told her. 'Always playing tricks and walking among us in disguise, so we don't know him.'

'And here,' said Akkikuyu with relish, 'is Mabb.'

The third card showed a female rat wearing a tasselled headdress. Her eyes were gold and painted in the centre of her brows was a third, the symbol of hidden power and sorcery.

Klakkweena bowed and again traced a circle on her own forehead in veneration.

'She's the sleep visitor,' she told Fleabee in a reverent voice. 'The dream haunter, who inspires her

followers to war and makes them bold, filling their hearts with courage.'

'She is the consort of Hobb,' Madame Akkikuyu added. 'Very powerful is Mabb. Guardian of all night magic.'

'They're not real though?' Fleabee said doubtfully. 'They're only legends, aren't they?'

The other rats sucked the air in sharply and Akkikuyu clutched at one of her amulets.

'More real than you!' she exclaimed. 'In times gone by, Lord Hobb he worshipped all over, his followers fill the forests.'

'So where are the Three now then? What happened to them?'

'Squirrels happened,' Klakkweena spat. 'Them dirty tree-huggers in Greenwich did fer Hobb. Cast a spell on him and locked him in a prison, they did. But he'll break out one day. Then they'll be sorry – all of 'em – yes, even Jupiter.'

'And what about Mabb? Where is she?'

'She and Bauchan, they wait for Hobb,' the fortune-teller said. 'Their deep magic sleeps, but it is waking, it is waking.'

Taking hold of Fleabee's claw, Akkikuyu looked into her eyes. 'It is Mabb you must entreat. Ask for help, ratlet – she will aid you.'

'How do I do that? How do I find her?'

Akkikuyu took the three cards from her, returned them to the pack then disappeared inside the tent for a moment.

When she returned she was carrying a small sacking pillow.

''Ere!' Klakkweena cried, smacking her knees in surprise. 'That there's a Mabb Rest! Not seen one of them since the days of Old Manky.'

Madame Akkikuyu nodded and gave it to Fleabee. ''Tis filled with herbs and the flower of broad bean,' she explained. 'The head that goes sleepy on this, she have visions and dreams. Mabb will come to you, young ratlet – she will speak and tell you what to do.'

Fleabee accepted the pillow nervously. The symbol of the third eye was painted on it. Was this really the answer to her troubles?

'Does Mabb speak to you?' she asked.

Akkikuyu chuckled. 'Oh yes,' she lied. 'Many chats we have.'

Klakkweena regarded her with renewed awe. She believed in the Raith Sidhe absolutely and gladly held out the bag with the peanuts as payment.

The black rat reached out to take them but faltered. Glancing at Fleabee clinging to the pillow and hugging it to her breast, her hopes fixed upon it and trusting all that she had heard, a twinge of regret stole into Akkikuyu's toughened heart. She could see how desperate the youngster was, for this night could very well be her last.

A desolate coldness washed over the fortune-teller. She remembered what it was like to be Fleabee's age, with such innocent faith in the deceits of others.

'No charge,' she said unexpectedly. 'Mabb Rest is gift.'

Klakkweena wondered if she had heard correctly but was assured that she had.

'Thank you,' Fleabee cried. 'Thank you so much.'

Madame Akkikuyu could not bear her gratitude. 'Go now,' she spluttered. 'Talk over. Back to sewers, you hurry.'

'Nowt fer you to worry about now,' Klakkweena told her daughter. 'Mabb will see you right, she'll protect you.'

Fleabee could have wept with joy. The awful weight that had been crushing her was lifted. Madame Akkikuyu had sold her tale too well. She truly believed that the ancient Goddess of the rats would visit her that very night and all her problems would be solved.

She was about to walk away with her mother when she ran back and gave the fortune-teller a grateful hug.

The black rat cringed and uttered a pained cry as though she had been wounded.

'Come,' Klakkweena said urgently. 'Sooner you get to sleep the better.'

Standing by the entrance of her tent, Madame Akkikuyu was trembling. She had done many foul and heinous deeds in the past, but this was one of the worst.

Watching the sewer rats depart, the knowledge that nothing would happen that night was an agony to her.

'Poor little ratlet,' she murmured, aghast. 'So simple, so young. What has Akkikuyu done? Akkikuyu no go down to Firstblood tomorrow. She pack and leave at first light.'

And she disappeared into the tent to weep silent, lonely tears.

9
Sleep Visitors

Fleabee and Klakkweena hurried back to the sewers.

'Don't you say nowt to no one about where we been,' the ratwife said sternly as they slithered down the rusted railing. 'And keep real quiet about that Mabb Rest.'

'Scabmona will see it,' Fleabee told her. 'I won't be able to hide it from her.'

'Then I'll have to bribe her somehow, no use threatenin' that one. Good job we still got these 'ere peanuts!'

When they reached the main tunnel of the rat domain they found that the row between Hagnakker and Fletch was still raging and had drawn quite a crowd.

'What a raterwauling spot o' entertainment,' cackled an old rat. 'I does enjoy a rompin' scrap. How many times she biffed him now?'

'More'n fourteen,' a scrawny crone informed him.

'How much more?'

'I dunno, I can't count more'n fourteen.'

Klakkweena and her daughter squeezed by unnoticed and scurried to their own rat hole.

Rancid Alf was snoring loudly. Fleabee went straight to her bed and solemnly placed the pillow down with an air of ceremony. The symbol of the third eye was uppermost and she traced the design with her claws, closing her own eyes and wishing with all her heart to be shown the way out of the ordeal that awaited her.

Carrying a candle, Klakkweena looked in on her and glanced at the slumbering Scabmona sceptically.

'Jump into bed and get that sleep,' she advised Fleabee in an urgent whisper, as she turned to leave. 'In the morning I wants to hear what She said to you!'

Fleabee clambered into her nest and gently smoothed the sacking of the pillow before resting her head upon it.

Just as she was about to lie down, Scabmona's voice came to her from the darkness.

'What does Old Klakk think I'm going to say to you?' she demanded.

'She didn't mean you.'

'Who then?'

'It doesn't matter.'

'I reckon the pair of you are barmy. So where've you been?'

'Nowhere.'

'Suit yerselves. What's that you've got?'

'A pillow, that's all.'

Scabmona gurgled with scornful laughter. 'You really are cracked as a smashed egg,' she hooted.

'Leave me alone. I need to sleep.'

'You know tomorrow night?'

'What about it?'

'You're so gonna get doofered.'

And Scabmona chuckled herself back to sleep.

Fleabee eased herself down. The Mabb Rest was soft under her cheek and she turned to face the wall. It had been a long day and a thrilling night for her. She thought of the bright patterns that the Flying Mongolians had created with their torches and the fussing ways of their hamster manager. The image of Madame Akkikuyu appeared in a hail of sparks, swimming beneath the lids of her eyes, and she snuggled herself down.

Her pink nose wrinkled and twitched. The herbs

and dried flowers that stuffed the Mabb Rest were fragrant and whispered of balmy summer days in fields that she had never seen and the delicious shade of hawthorn hedges.

Returning to the claustrophobic sewers had been more difficult this time than the last. Fleabee's heart ached to venture further and leave this grim shadowy world behind. Surely life in the upper world was not as harsh as down here? She thought of Nuff the hamster again, and wondered what he had meant when he said he had been a captive? From whose prison had he and the gerbils escaped? Why did Klakkweena tell her to have nothing to do with bats? Perhaps life was just as hard up there after all. Akkikuyu had said that the world was a bad place. Was there a God who ruled the great outside just as cruelly as Jupiter reigned in the sewers?

These thoughts churned through her mind and after some time Fleabee realised that she was not in the least bit tired. And then a new worry struck her. What if she never slept at all that night? Madame Akkikuyu's gift would be wasted. She began to fret and became even more wide-awake.

Curling herself into a ball, she squeezed her eyes tightly shut and tried to force herself to go to sleep. After several minutes, the strain of it became unbearable and her eyes snapped open.

The dark pressed close around her and she sighed. The rat hole was filled with the sound of others sleeping. Scabmona's snuffling piggy snores were droning close by. Outside the room, the fruity snout gargles of Rancid Alf were trumpeting away, alongside the phlegm-driven croaking of Klakkweena.

In the tunnel beyond, the waters were sluicing and drips plopped loudly from the brickwork, a drunken voice called out in anger, someone laughed scornfully and the echoes went ringing under the arched ceiling – away into a distorted distance. It was a typical night in Jupiter's nightmarish realm and the world was rolling by without a thought for her at this crucial time.

Fleabee groaned and turned over. Why couldn't she find sleep?

She closed her eyes again and waited.

'No time for sleep, Child,' said a sudden voice.

Fleabee sat up in alarm.

Someone was sitting at the end of her bed!

She could just make out the bulky shape of a large rat. Had he been sent by Morgan to doofer her now? Such things had been known.

'Wha …what do you want?' she stuttered, pulling the ragged blankets up to her chin.

The rat shook his head sadly. 'Look at her,' he said, his face turned to where Scabmona was sleeping noisily. 'What a woe-begotten terror. So fierce, so full of hate and malice. What a hideous place this is.'

Fleabee could not believe her ears. The stranger's voice was gentle and filled with compassion. He was not criticising Scabmona but grieving for the circumstances that had created her and lamenting for what she might have been.

'Who are you?' she asked, her fears subsiding.

'Don't you know?' he said, with a warm and kind chuckle in his voice. 'Have you not guessed?'

A preposterous, impossible thought flashed across Fleabee's mind.

'No,' she breathed.

'You must leave this awful place,' he told her. 'Only death and misery flourish here. Your family is wretched and beyond redemption. Leave this foulness far behind. For your own sweet sake.'

Fleabee could not make out the rat's features in the darkness but for an instant she caught a glint of green deep in his eyes.

'What's your name?' she murmured.

'You know it already,' came the kindly reply. 'And I thank you for the comforting words you said unto me today.'

As he spoke, a faint radiance began to glimmer, a beautiful emerald glow that steadily welled up, branching over the walls until at last his face was revealed.

Fleabee gasped.

'Scabmona!' she cried. 'Wake up! Look!'

The rat smiled benevolently. 'She will not wake, Child,' he said. 'I have not been sent to her.'

Fleabee looked at him in stunned amazement.

The rat had a friendly, honest face. A bright sparkle was in his eyes, which were set deep beneath a care-worn brow. Around his snout his grizzled fur grew long and curly and from his chin sprouted a short wavy beard. He looked very like the image that had been carved of him many years ago.

'But it can't be,' Fleabee said. 'You … you're dead.'

The ghost of 'Orace Baldmony chuckled softly. 'Don't be afraid,' he told her.

'I'm not afraid. Just … a bit … shocked. You're not who I was expecting. And … you don't look like how I imagined a ghost would look.'

'Orace laughed. 'I suppose you thought I'd be all see-through and smoky? That really would have frightened you.'

'But why are you here?'

'I've come to help.'

'How can you help me?'

'Watch,' he said simply.

'Orace raised his claws and the light that had been slowly spreading throughout the room suddenly burst into vibrant life. Bright colours swept by and a warm breeze laced with the perfume of countless flowers and blossom rushed around her.

Swaying shapes began to form and the bricks seemed to shrink back and melt away, until Fleabee was surrounded by a meadow of verdant grass, rippling like the sea.

With a rattle of falling mortar, the ceiling of her room spun off into a star-crowded sky. The full moon shone down, its beams of shimmering silver, and the fragrant air was filled with the rush of the wind and the rustle of great trees.

'Orace motioned for her to stand and, staring

incredulously about her, the ratgirl obeyed.

The brown feathers of the mallard which she wore about her neck stirred in the gentle wind and when 'Orace playfully waved his claw over them they shone with new, rainbow colours.

'Where are we?' Fleabee breathed. 'It's not the sewers, it's not even Deptford.'

'Only a small corner of the country,' the spirit answered. 'A little back-water far away from your gruesome den. There are many pockets like this in the world, my Child. Havens where the Green Mouse is revered.'

'The Green Mouse? I've never heard of that.'

'Walk with me and I'll explain,' he told her.

'Orace took her by the claw and led her through the grass. Fleabee took a last look back at the sleeping Scabmona, then followed gladly.

'For many years,' the ghost began, 'I was Jupiter's henchrat and chief lackey, like Morgan is now. Just as cruel as him I was, because I believed in those great fiery eyes in the portal and knew no different. Then one day some of the lads went on a raid and fetched back a whole crowd of mice. I won't tell you what we did to them and I weep to recall it now. But one of them mouses was earmarked for my own nasty pleasure. A real baddun I was, they didn't come much worse than me. In those days I used to taunt

162

my victims, make 'em wait and listen to their tormented cries.'

He paused and sniffed away a tear. 'But this one mousey, instead of snivellin' and squealin' for his life as so many did before, what he does is pray to the Green. Asks Him to find it in His great heart to forgive me, he does. I wasn't having none of that, so I demanded to know what game he was playing at and why he wasn't as proper scared and mortified as he ought to be.'

Their footsteps led them through the grassy meadow to a field of golden barleycorn and Fleabee gradually became aware of many voices raised in happy song.

'Orace grinned. 'Listen to that,' he said. 'Don't it lift your soul? That's the sound of joy and the noise of those happy to be alive. You don't hear that down the sewers.'

'No,' Fleabee agreed. 'Never.'

A pathway formed by the passage of countless small feet led into the cornfield. With the tall barley rising high on either side, Fleabee followed her strange guide along it and the sound of the singing grew steadily closer.

'Carry on with your story,' she said. 'Why wasn't that mouse frightened?'

The ghost heaved a wistful sigh. 'He told me he wasn't scared because the Green Mouse would watch over him, even after he were dead and gone. And he wasn't talking about no green mouldy mouse corpse – oh no.'

'What then?'

'Orace threw open his arms to embrace all that was around them. 'He is the essence of Spring,' he began. 'The indomitable force within every living, growing thing. In every new bud, there He is, in every gentle rainfall and each ray of life-giving light. And, when I heard what that small brave mouse had to say as he waited for me to peel him, something thawed in my sinful old heart. I let that mouse go free and tried to make the sewers a better place.'

His voice trailed off and his forehead creased before continuing. 'But Jupiter wouldn't stand for that,' he said at length. 'He soon guessed what I was up to and the only thing I could do was escape. I knew he'd send my own lads after me and in my terror I prayed to the Green to save me. It was then that I found it, that Grille and the cellar where lots of mice were living.

'They'd never had any dealings with sewer folk before and welcomed me in, not realising the danger I brought with me. They told me more of the Green Mouse and I sang their songs with them and for the first time in my wicked, wasted life I actually liked who I was. I wanted to stay with my new friends forever.'

He lowered his eyes. 'But you don't get away from

Jupiter that easy,' he said. 'It wasn't long till the lads found their old lieutenant and my little mouse friends paid dear for their welcome of me. I was made to watch it all and then it were my turn. I didn't give that misguided crew what they wanted, though. I wouldn't cry out and beg for a quick end. I sang the songs the mice had learned me and that's how I died.'

'I'm sorry,' Fleabee said.

'Orace looked at her and the green glow shone keenly in his eyes. 'Don't be,' he laughed, and he performed a skipping jig. 'That brief time I spent with my new friends was the best of my life and I was free of Jupiter at last.'

The narrow path veered left and began to slope downwards. They had come to the edge of the field and the barley grew less densely around them.

Fleabee shielded her eyes. Shafts of brilliant green light were streaming towards her, raking through the corn stems in slender beams.

'What is it?' she asked.

'You'll see,' 'Orace told her. 'Almost there.'

The singing and the sound of merry voices was louder now. When the last of the barley stems had been passed and her shadow stretched far behind along the path, Fleabee's eyes adjusted to the glare and a broad smile lit her face.

They were standing on a mossy bank that dipped

gently down to a wide pool, fringed with willow trees. A small island was at the centre and upon this, stretching high into the heavens, was a wondrous oak. It was untouched by the chills of March, for it was heavy with the luxuriant foliage of high summer. Hundreds of silver lanterns hung from the shapely branches and the green flames that burned in them cast a delicious, nourishing light in every direction. It was the most magical, enchanting sight Fleabee had ever seen.

The pool was not deserted.

A host of other animals were rejoicing in the Green's splendour. Fieldmice were wading up to their middles and splashing each other, delighting in the emerald fires which blazed gloriously in every droplet. A trio of hedgehogs was watching and tittering to themselves as they gingerly immersed their prickly bodies. Near the shore, a family of badgers was paddling and giving rides to a band of shrews while some adventurous rabbits were daring one another to swim. Stoats and weasels were swinging from the drooping willow branches and leaping out into the deep water to great applause; and voles were busily ferrying the smaller creatures across to the island, to marvel at the oak and climb up into the leaves.

Those animals whose voices were not raised in laughter or spluttering as a weasel dived into the pool close by, were singing in praise of the Green Mouse. It was a blissful, harmonious scene and one that Fleabee would never forget.

'What is this place?' she asked in a hushed whisper.

'Orace was letting the light play over his face. He closed his eyes and lifted his head back to offer up a silent prayer before answering.

'It's where weary hearts come to be refreshed,' he said. 'Where the lonely and dejected are revived and the sorrowful given hope for the new day.'

'It isn't real though, is it?'

'Real enough for them,' he told her, nodding at the joyous revellers. 'In the morning they'll awaken with the strength to do what they must.'

'Look!' cried a young fieldmouse when he saw Fleabee and 'Orace standing at the water's edge.

Everyone turned to face them and the ratgirl suddenly felt shy and awkward.

'Welcome!' a rabbit called. 'Join us!'

The call was taken up and soon they were all imploring her to enter the pool.

'Orace chuckled and ambled into the water, grinning widely as it rose to his knees.

Fleabee hesitated and the ghost turned around to encourage her. 'It's lovely and warm,' he said. 'Just follow me, Child. A few more steps and you will be cleansed of Jupiter's world forever. Let the Grace and watchful presence of the Green Mouse be with you. All your fears will wash away.'

'I don't feel right,' she demurred. 'I don't belong here.'

'You belong here more than most,' 'Orace said earnestly. 'Your heart is sore with troubles. Come, ease the cares that pain you. Be at peace this night and know what it is to be loved.'

Fleabee gazed about her. The animals looked so cheerful and free of worry. She longed to cast aside the chains that bound her thoughts and she took a faltering step to the water's edge.

'That's it,' 'Orace beckoned. 'A little more and you can throw off your sadness.'

'Stay,' a husky, female voice called suddenly.

Fleabee halted.

The voice had come from the cornfield behind her.

A look of concern stole over 'Orace's face.

'Who is there?' Fleabee asked, shifting round to look at the swaying barley.

'Do not go into the water,' the hidden stranger continued. 'Wait for me.'

'Orace shivered and cried out quickly, 'Fleabee! Hurry, join us!'

But the ratgirl wanted to see who this newcomer was. The voice was deep and resonant. She peered beyond the golden stems.

A tall shape was moving in the corn, a stealthy,

graceful figure, and where it trod the green light was dimmed and shadow poured into its wake.

Closer it came, approaching with steady purpose and Fleabee caught quick glimpses of a rat shape wearing a large headdress festooned with orange and crimson ribbons.

'Child!' 'Orace cried desperately. 'You are in peril. Step into the pool while there is yet time!'

Fleabee could feel her heart beating faster. The figure in the field was very near now. A warm, sulphurous wind blew from the barley and the ribbons on the headdress were writhing like burning serpents. Then she saw a pair of deep golden eyes flare in the gloom and knew who it was.

Mabb was here.

The ratgirl was not sure whether to be pleased or afraid. There was a slow, assured menace about the figure and its coaxing voice. Not wishing to see any more, Fleabee whirled around to face 'Orace again.

The other animals in the pool were whimpering unhappily and covering their faces.

'No!' they wept as the dark Goddess of the Raith Sidhe emerged from the field.

The sumptuous green light wavered and sickened.

'Save us!' the animals sobbed.

'Orace held out his claws. 'Swiftly!' he told Fleabee. 'The Green Mouse will protect you!'

Fleabee moved to the water but, before she could even dip in her toes, the rich, sultry voice of Mabb commanded her to stop.

'Hold girl!' she called. 'Why do you fear me and try to escape? It was you who invoked me this night. I have come at your summons, will you not hear my words?'

'Orace shook his head at Fleabee. 'Do not listen!' he warned. 'She will deceive and use you!'

Mabb gave a low, indulgent laugh. 'Deceit and use!' she scorned. 'They are the devices of your precious Green. His agents are fed with smiles and promises yet he spends them freely enough when it suits him. The Three do not sacrifice our own, get you gone – back to the empty void, quivering phantom of an ignoble traitor!'

'Never!' 'Orace defied her. 'You shall not have this one!'

'She is already mine,' Mabb's voice rapped back. 'She was mine at her birth, born unto me in mine own stars.'

Fleabee's skin crawled. She did not have the courage to turn her head and see the apparition that was now standing close behind her. She could feel the hot breath beating on her neck, where every hair tingled and rose.

'Don't listen to her,' 'Orace cried. 'She is the Mother of Lies. The Green is good and you owe her nothing.'

Fleabee tried to move but when she lowered her eyes to look into the water at her feet, she saw her own petrified face reflected. And there standing behind her, with the ribbons of her pagan headdress flying and her gold eyes glinting with power, was Mabb. Fleabee was frozen with fear.

'Please Child,' 'Orace pleaded. 'For your safety's sake, join me.'

'Silence old one,' Mabb declared, and the ghost fell back into the water, pushed by an unseen force.

'I will be heard,' she growled. 'For nearly a thousand years I have slept and tonight this girl has roused me from that slumber. I will be heard!'

'You're evil through and through!' 'Orace shouted. 'A devil of the dark past. You have no place here now!

Return to the Pit where you belong and roast there for eternity – leave this world in peace!'

A gale of harsh mocking laughter blew about the pool and the barley bowed and buckled before the force of it. Fleabee clenched her teeth as her hair lashed about her ears and her fur felt as though it were combed by knives.

'Peace!' Mabb bellowed. 'What peace is there in this world? War rages more savagely now than when the Three Thrones were raised in the one forest of old, at the beginning of days. This world is more than ready and ripe for our return and mighty have we grown in our long slumber!'

'Never!' 'Orace cried. 'You shall not get a foothold in the waking world again. The Green will stop you!'

'Gullible zealot!' she sneered. 'The Green has not the strength to withstand us.'

Goaded to anger and anxious to pull Fleabee from danger, 'Orace rushed forward. But the eyes of Mabb flared at him and he was thrown back into the pool again, where he floundered in the deep water.

The other animals swam to help him and their frightened, panic-stricken cries drew more laughter from Mabb's lips.

'This weak and credulous rabble is no company for you,' she said in Fleabee's ear. 'I know what it is you crave most, you are my creature – dedicated to my service at the hour of your birth. I know your innermost desires – those secret yearnings that have dripped into the hidden chambers of your heart for as long as you can recall. I know what you long for, I know what hope glows in your veins, the hope that Jupiter could not overcome by his artless sorcery.'

'What…what is that?' Fleabee stuttered.

'You wish for freedom. To be who you are with no one controlling you. It is in my power to give that to you, Girl. Will you hearken to my words?'

Fleabee stared at 'Orace and the others, still struggling in the pool.

'No!' the ghost called out to her. 'Deny her!'

Fleabee swallowed nervously and closed her eyes so she could not see him. 'I'll listen,' she muttered guiltily.

The hot breath fanned her neck as Mabb laughed.

'You choose with wisdom,' she said. 'I will show you a way out of those squalid sewers and your pointless existence there. A new life is opening for you. If you honour me and become my priestess then nothing will be withheld from you. Power will be yours and knowledge also. Magical secrets unknown even to Jupiter the Usurper I will tell to you. You who were born in the sign of the Ratwitch, in the House of Mabb, does this sound good to you?'

Fleabee took a deep breath and nodded slowly. 'Yes,' she replied.

'So be it! She has chosen!'

A strong claw clamped on her shoulder. The air was split with thunder and the stars were blotted out by swiftly rolling storm clouds that rumbled over the sky.

A fork of lightning came crashing from above and hit the earth with a blinding flash. There was an explosion of soil and moss. Then another jag of energy streaked out of the night. In an instant Fleabee was surrounded by a lethal net of dancing light.

The surface of the pool began to churn and the animals wailed in fear and distress. Spouts of water shot upwards and the frightened creatures battled to reach the island and the far shore.

A clap of thunder shook the ground and the willows creaked as the squall tore into them. Leaves were stripped from the branches and filled the tormented air. Stinging rain hammered down and the lanterns in the oak were swiftly quenched.

Darkness swallowed the island. The animals who threw themselves at the great tree clung to it desperately, praying to the Green Mouse. But their voices were lost in the fury of the tempest.

Only Mabb's voice could be heard, laughing above the thunder and the shaking of the world. Bolts of lightning blasted into the cornfield and hungry flames leaped up. Columns of black smoke were whisked by the battering gale, and greedy fires ripped through the barley.

Fighting against the destroying storm, the ghost of 'Orace Baldmony stumbled his way to the bank.

'Begone!' he yelled, holding out his arms in a gesture of defiance. 'Chaos and death is all you bring!'

'Hobb will return!' the Goddess declared. 'The Three will rule once more! There is nothing you or all your pathetic, happy singing can do to prevent it.'

'Maybe I can't,' 'Orace bawled back at her. 'But this Child can, or you would not need her so badly!'

Turning a rain-lashed face to Fleabee, he reached out his claws to her.

'Don't do this, Child,' he begged. 'Don't do what this monster wants! Would you supplant one tyrant with three more?'

Fleabee was shaking. She felt as though she had betrayed poor 'Orace but she could not refuse what Mabb had offered. This was the only way out for her.

'I'm sorry,' she said, shamefully.

Mabb laughed, her eyes flashed and 'Orace was plucked from the ground. High into the air he was flung and, spinning head over tail, into the darkness he went, wailing.

' 'Orace!' Fleabee cried. 'Oh why did you do that?'

'Pay him no heed,' Mabb told her. 'This is but a dream and is he not already dead? That cowardly fool was the only one of his kind ever to have prayed to the Green Mouse and yet he still let him be killed.'

'What about the others?' Fleabee demanded. 'The fieldmice and the rest?'

'In the deathly hours of the night,' Mabb said with a drawl, 'they will wake with a start. Cold yet sweating from this memory, they will offer up worthless supplications to their beloved Green. What use is there in grovelling to a spent force, a power that is unable to save you when you are in your direst need? Prayers should be answered. Every word uttered in my name finds my ears. When you are my high priestess, you will know this to be true.'

Behind them the field was burning fiercely and the wall of heat that beat from it singed the fur on Fleabee's back and scorched her tail. Before her the pool was seething and white foaming waves rushed up the shore on either side of her. The oak groaned beneath the storm, a mighty bough splintered and toppled into the fuming water.

Disaster and nightmare raged all around. It was as if the end of the world had come.

'Come,' Mabb cried. 'Arise with me.'

The claw tightened on Fleabee's shoulder and the lightning blasted more ferociously. Earth, water and flame erupted into the night and then to Fleabee's astonishment, she felt herself lifting off the ground. Up above the burning field and seething pool she flew, scattering the choking smoke of the fire and soaring up towards the violent clouds.

Into the tortured heavens she rose and in her ear, Mabb's persuasive voice poured miraculous promises.

'Look below you,' she instructed. 'See how the world shall be.'

Fleabee stared down at the dwindling land. The cornfield was now a blackened stretch of smoking stubble and the fire had moved on to devour the neighbouring meadow. The pool was defiled with soil, ashes and uprooted willow trees, and the oak had been struck by lightning and was burning furiously.

'I don't want that,' she cried, with an angry shake of her head.

'Patience,' Mabb told her. 'This is but a passing frenzy. I have slept long and my powers are relishing their liberty. See beyond the ruined landscape of this dream. Down to that darksome place you hate most of all.'

As Fleabee watched, the field split apart and the earth yawned open. The pool spilled into the abyss and down in the unlit regions, further than the deepest delving roots of gnarled and ancient trees, the tunnels of the Deptford sewers were laid bare.

Thunder resounded in the sky and spears of lightning struck the abyss.

A tremendous crack fractured the crumbling brickwork. The labyrinthine sewers snapped open to reveal thousands of rats, teeming in the filthy water, darting in terror from the brutal downpour.

'What an insignificant, lowly region,' Mabb said. 'Jupiter must indeed be a paltry God to endure such base comforts as that allows. How can you bear to dwell in such a dank and dismal hole?'

'It's the only home I know,' Fleabee answered, 'And sometimes, when the light finds its way in, it's very beautiful down there.'

'Then it shall be yours to rule. When Jupiter is overthrown, the denizens of the sewers will be your subjects. Those that have jeered and mocked you throughout your life will be yours to command. The whole of that realm, and more, I will give to you gladly.'

Fleabee stared at the rats scrabbling for cover far below. No one would laugh at her any more or call her cruel names. She could not imagine a life without insults.

'What must I do?' she asked quickly.

Mabb laughed, and the hot breath moved close to her ear.

'The smallest of things,' she whispered. 'One simple act, then this and more will be yours. The Lord of the Raith Sidhe is imprisoned but the span of his confinement is nearly over. The way must be prepared for his return. The King of Night will soon be free. Will you aid us? Will you do this one slight thing for the Three who sat enthroned in majesty and power before the first mousebrass was ever forged, before the first squirrel took up the silver, before the bats knew of the moon-sent angel and before the great serpent writhed in the East?'

'Yes,' Fleabee breathed. 'I'll do it.'

A great claw reached around the ratgirl's head and traced upon her brow the sign of the third eye.

'Then let it be done, High Priestess of Mabb!' the voice burned in her ear.

With that the storm burst with renewed violence. The clouds boiled above and the world tilted and convulsed below. Lightning scarred the air and the thunder jolted her very bones.

'But what must I do?' Fleabee cried. 'What must I do?'

Only the howling gale answered. With the pelting rain stinging her eyes, she spun around and called out to Mabb, but she was gone.

Alone in the dark, whirling sky, Fleabee threw back her head. 'What must I do?' she yelled again.

'Oh shut your face,' barked a bad-tempered voice.

Fleabee sat up.

She was back in the rat hole and Scabmona was glaring at her.

10
Preparations

I s it morning?' Fleabee asked.

Her sister threw her a disgusted look. 'Yes,' she snapped. 'And you woke me up!'

Fleabee rubbed her eyes. 'I was dreaming,' she said.

Scabmona mumbled and scratched a scab she had been cultivating on her knee. Then she ate it and scrambled out of bed.

'Lot to do today anyways,' she said, with a wicked grin. 'It's Firstblood tonight. Just think, this time tomorrow this room will be all mine!'

Cackling gleefully, she bounced out in search of breakfast.

Fleabee remained in her bed, feeling drained and exhausted by everything that had happened in her dreams.

Klakkweena's quarrelsome voice was soon bawling at Scabmona. The usual morning squabble ensued and for once Rancid Alf was in accord with Klakkweena.

Scabmona was given a dry crust and told to make herself scarce.

An instant later Klakkweena shambled into the sleeping chamber and stared hopefully at Fleabee.

'Well?' she demanded. 'What did She say to you?'

'I'm not sure,' Fleabee answered.

Her mother scowled. 'What do you mean? How can you not be sure?'

'It was all so strange and frightening. I don't know what to think.'

'Tell me everything,' Klakkweena insisted, settling herself down on Scabmona's messy nest and rubbing her claws excitedly.

'But it was only a dream,' said Fleabee.

The ratwife grunted in exasperation. 'You stupid luggins! Mabb is the sleep visitor, that's how she speaks with her followers.'

'But what if a dream is all it was? How can I be certain?'

Klakkweena clicked her tongue in annoyance then pursed her lips. She reached across and flicked the duck feathers on the ratgirl's necklace.

'What happened here?' she asked. 'You choked a budgie and not told no one?'

Fleabee regarded the feathers in surprise. They were bright yellow, red, blue and green.

'That happened in my dream,' she breathed fearfully. 'So it was all true!'

Klakkweena sucked her bottom fang in rapture. 'Of course it was,' she squealed. 'Akkikuyu told you the Mabb Rest would work! Oh what a glut of jollies this day is! What did Mabb say?'

'You won't believe me.'

'Tell me, or I'll bite your nose off!'

Fleabee stared into her mother's eager eyes and took a deep breath. 'Mabb wants me to be her High Priestess,' she told her.

Klakkweena gaped at her.

'Mother?' Fleabee ventured after a long pause.

In silence Klakkweena rose and crossed to the doorway.

'Alf!' she roared.

'What does my baneful, wart-bottomed pixie desire?' came the answering call.

'Get out,' she ordered. 'Stand at the entrance, outside it mind you – and don't let no one in. You hear me?'

Rancid Alf came pattering to the sleeping chamber and looked at her blankly. 'What's all this?' he asked. 'You swallowed a bad nut? You got a face like a trodden slug.'

He peeped in at Fleabee but Klakkweena shooed

him away. 'Do as you're told,' she snapped, and so determined and frightful was her expression that Alf shuffled away with his tail between his legs.

When she was quite certain he was gone, Klakkweena came and sat beside her daughter.

'Now,' she said. 'Every detail.'

Fleabee lowered her eyes. She thought it best to leave out the parts concerning 'Orace Baldmony's ghost and recounted all that had happened from the moment Mabb had come prowling from the cornfield.

When she finished, she found that her mother was looking at her with a confused mixture of fear, wonder and dread.

'You do believe me, don't you?' Fleabee asked.

Klakkweena said nothing. She cast about the room as if searching for an answer, then reverently picked up the Mabb Rest and held it tightly.

'All these years,' she murmured. 'All these years, I knew – I believed in Her. When I was a ratling I spoke to her in the dark and wept my very last secret tears to her. Why didn't she come to me? Why choose you?'

Fleabee shook her head. 'I don't know,' she said apologetically. 'I haven't a clue why. I'm useless – everyone knows that. I've heard it all my life.'

Laying the pillow on her lap, her mother put her arm around her and with a trembling, unpractised claw, groomed Fleabee's fringe behind her ears. It was the most tender demonstration of her love that she had ever expressed.

'Only once,' she began a little clumsily. 'I'll say this one time only, so never ask to hear it again – 'cos I'll deny it was ever said. Though you've caused me nowt but shame and disgrace, I ...'

The ratwife paused and cleared her throat, as though the words had lodged in there like a splintered chicken bone.

'I,' she resumed, 'I was never anything but proud of you.'

'P ... Proud of me? Why?'

'Because you never gave in,' Klakkweena confessed, with a gentle smile that softened her belligerent face. 'Not once were you anything 'cept what you wanted to be. In spite of all the bullying and beatings, the screaming and the threats, you stood your ground and didn't waver. In that way you was braver than the whole accursed lot of us. To fly against everyone, the way you have, takes more guts than I ever had. If you've had it tough, maybe it's 'cos I was extra hard on you – to see how steely you really was. And, though I swore and bruised you, I was never disappointed, not once.'

Fleabee buried her face in her mother's breast and sobbed.

'That's why you've been chosen,' Klakkweena said,

holding her tightly. 'Among this scurvy mob of cut-throats, wasters and swaggering vipers, you're the strongest. Don't you see? Who else would the Raith Sidhe choose to serve them? No one but my Fleabee would do, there ain't nobody better.'

For several minutes they hugged each other, both forgetting for that single time that they were Jupiter's subjects and lived in a realm where such affection was unknown and reviled.

'I don't even know what I'm supposed to do for Mabb,' Fleabee finally said. 'How will I know?'

'Trust in Her, Fleabee. That's another thing only you could do. Somehow, you'll be shown the ...'

Klakkweena's voice died in her throat and she stifled a cry of surprise.

Fleabee jumped up, thinking that Scabmona had put a vicious spider in the bed.

Klakkweena was pointing at the place on the bed where the Mabb Rest had been and when Fleabee followed her fixed gaze, she too gasped and covered her mouth.

Lying upon the rags was a small, curved knife.

It was a beautiful but deadly-looking blade. The handle was carved in bone and bound in gleaming gold, inscribed with strange letters. Set into the middle and resembling a great drop of twilight was a large amethyst that formed the sign of the third eye.

'A gift from Mabb,' Klakkweena murmured. 'Oh Fleabee, I could spit ten shades of phlegm, I'm that staggered and fit to bust!'

'What do I need a special knife for?' her daughter asked uncertainly.

Klakkweena rocked backward and cackled in delight. 'It's the blade of a High Priestess,' she said. 'A sign that Mabb is watching over you. Pick it up.'

'Why don't you?'

'Because it's not meant fer me. I daresn't touch it, not for all the grease in London.'

Fleabee gingerly took up the knife. The handle fitted snugly in her palm and the blade glittered with a frosty light when she gave the air an experimental jab.

'You don't have no worries no more,' Klakkweena told her. 'You'll breeze through Firstblood. Mabb'll see to it. Just keep that pretty spiker with you.'

'I will,' Fleabee answered grimly. 'What choice do I have?'

Scabmona spent a very enjoyable morning. First of all she occupied herself by rampaging into other rat holes: stealing whatever she could lay her claws on, smacking babies and setting fire to the hair of an old crone who was still fast asleep, then being the first to hurl a bowl of sewer water over her to douse it.

It was a satisfying start to this special day and, chewing messily on stolen scraps, she strolled about the tunnels hunting for trouble.

Preparations for the approaching night were already underway. Scavenging parties had been given special permission by Morgan to venture above ground to fetch food for the feast and the privileged rats went scampering away in the highest of spirits.

Scabmona watched them race off and wondered about following them. Would she have more fun in the upper world than down here all day?

Rancid Alf and his idle gang were one of the lucky groups and the ratling ran after him for the entire length of the main tunnel, pestering them to let her join their expedition.

Her father yelled at her, Flake kicked her, Vinegar Pete said something sour and Leering Macky squinted in so many directions she wasn't sure who he was looking at.

Scabmona leaned sulkily against the wall as they disappeared around the corner, then a mischievous grin flashed on her face. Feeling very pleased with herself, she examined the mouse peeler that she had artfully 'lifted' from Macky's belt and sauntered back to the rat domain, whistling tunelessly to herself.

The feast was to be held in a large sewer where a wide platform provided ample space for the gruesome festivities.

A vile stench flowed out from it. Several ratwives had evidently commenced brewing an intoxicating, stomach-rotting beverage. That always went down well. Rancid Alf and Klakkweena were both partial to it.

Scabmona followed her nose and took an incurious look.

Some of the other ratlings were daubing crude faces and horrific scenes on the walls, with black and red paint that had been found on a tip by the first of the scrounging parties.

Scabmona viewed their artistic efforts with a contemptuous eye and told each one that there wasn't enough blood in the picture or it was nowhere near scary enough.

Her criticisms were met with jeers and arguments but she only laughed in their silly faces. Then, seizing a neglected brush and loading it with black paint she sloshed it across their art, splattered any ratlings who jumped at her and finished by kicking the paint pots over.

Guffawing, she skipped away, halting only to push Winjeela headlong into the oozing paint slick.

It was turning out to be rather a good day.

The hours skimmed by. Morning bled into the afternoon and the early evening descended.

In the chamber of Jupiter, an audience was coming to an end. The fiery eyes within the portal blazed once more with malice before receding, and the Lord of the Sewers crawled down into the invisible blackness of His lair.

Morgan was grovelling on his face before the altar candles and remained prostrate for many minutes before daring to rise.

With a wary glance into the dark archway, the Cornish rat scurried along the ledge to an opening in the wall. A small ante-room lay beyond where, for nearly four hundred years, the lieutenants of Jupiter had slept in order to be at the constant beck and call of their tyrannical master.

Sitting on a low stool, Wormy Ned was absorbed in adding entries to his book when Morgan entered, in a foul temper.

'Summat's up,' the piebald rat cursed. 'Did you hear Him just now? Summat's up, I tell you.'

Wormy Ned stuck the quill he had been writing with into his greasy hair and blew on the freshly inked page.

'I didn't catch much of it,' he said, between puffs. 'I was totting up bribes and speculating who's next fer the chop. But from the bits I did hear, He didn't sound none too happy.'

Morgan licked his fangs

and shuddered. 'He weren't. Says He feels some other presence in His realm, some other power and He won't have it.'

'What sort of other power?'

'How the stink should I know? He wouldn't tell me. But whatever it is, it's bit Him real bad. Ain't never known Him like that before. Not in all my years of service. Gave me a real blisterin' – thought I was gonna be dragged in and eaten, I did.'

Wormy Ned tried to reassure him. 'Our Glorious Emperor of Despair wouldn't do that. He knows how loyal you are and how much you does fer Him.'

'There's always another who'll pounce into the breach,' Morgan spat. 'Some other likely bit of filth who'll chance his claw to be the new lieutenant. That One-Eyed Jake fancies himself as a boss, I've seen it in him, and he's been makin' himself popular with the lads of late. Aye, there's him and many another treacherous rebel I could name.'

He glowered at Ned but the small rat laughed off the accusation. 'I don't want your job,' he swore. 'I'd not have time for the book-keeping.'

'Mebbe,' Morgan muttered, pacing about the room. 'But these are unsettling times. I feel it in me bones, the stump of me tail is itchin' and that ain't happened since it were hacked off when I was a callous youth.'

'What you need is a swig of gut-rot and be at the

front of the chase tonight. That'd put the snap back in your whiskers. I've marked you down for baggin' a brace of them ratlings.'

Morgan frowned. 'A bit of sport would go a long ways to easin' this naggin' doubt,' he admitted. 'But fer an awful minute back there I thought He was gonna forbid this Firstblood.'

Wormy Ned closed the book and shook his ink-blotted head. 'He wouldn't do that, would He?' he cried. 'I got me registers ready to tick off who's gonna get spiked and there's all them wagers that've been laid. Why, there's been a Firstblood every year since…well as far back as the records go and that's almost two hundred and fifty years but it'd been going on a lot longer before that.'

'Keep yer nibs on,' Morgan told him. 'Tonight's still a go. When I said the lads wouldn't be happy, He went all quiet and whispery. There's summat goin' on, I tell you. Him in there has summat planned, some big job He ain't told us about yet is brewin'. He needs to keep the lads sweet. I don't like it.'

Wormy Ned poked the cork back into his bottle of ink. 'Don't matter whether you likes it or not,' he said. 'He'll tell you when He's good and ready and not before and then you'll do as you're told, just as always, just as the rest of us down here do. That's the poxy way of it.'

'Let's get this night cranked up and started then,'

Morgan muttered. 'I got a mighty thirst on me, and the fun and games are gonna be the best there's been fer a long space of years. I've already seen to that and you'd best set me down fer more than a brace of ratlings, I've got a hankering for enough skins to carpet this 'ere place. And one of them is gonna be that Sickweed daughter of Klakkweena's.'

With his stumpy tail thrashing behind him, Jupiter's lieutenant went marching from the ante-room and, hopping from the stool with the book under his arm, Wormy Ned scampered after.

11

Firstblood

Through the main tunnels strode Morgan and Wormy Ned, and every rat who met them stood aside to let them pass. They were all getting ready for the festivities and great excitement charged the stale air.

The scavenging parties had returned some time ago and an enormous spread of loathsome food had been laid out. It was a revolting buffet that only a rat could look at, let alone eat. No one could recall there ever being such a quantity and variety of dishes before.

There were the customary appetisers: fat bluebottles on sticks, a slime dip, gristle nibbles, the aptly named but tricky to eat crawling pie, assorted bones to gnaw at, nameless lump stew, maggot pasties, a mound of sweaty luncheon meat that had been ripped into jaw-cramming chunks and strips of green ham. But there were other, more imaginative culinary additions this year.

A large bowl contained grey potato squelch covered in an impressive coating of blotchy green mould, there were frogspawn tartlets, humming cheese and fluffy toffee squeezeballs drizzled with an unidentifiable goo, lice fancies, sour milk and furry tomato trifle, a bowl of Flake's skin scratchings and sticky snotty pudding.

Most impressive of all however was the sight of seven goldfish that had been speared in a garden pond. Lightly roasted and still impaled, they gave the feast a very grand and opulent air.

For the assembled rats this ghastly banquet was an agonising, mouth-watering temptation but no one dared to even approach it. At Firstblood, the gorging could not commence until the chief henchrat had

had his fill and given the signal. Any transgression of this rule of Ratiquette would automatically mean being added to the menu.

When Lickit appeared, suitably armed for the night's trial, he stared at this festering abundance with unbelieving eyes and his long tongue unravelled down his chin as his mouth dropped open. From then on, till he eventually dived into the display and sated his appetite, his tongue dripped like a broken tap and his stomach gurgled like a drain.

Ratwives had made special efforts to look even more grotesque than usual and succeeded admirably. Fur was given fresh coats of sludge, the blood of squished beetles had been smeared around mouths and charcoal applied about the eyes, to startling effect. Those with hair had tortured it into new dramatic shapes and threaded as much outrageous decoration into it as possible.

Hagnakker's matted, twig-stuck locks were the envy of many. She had ornamented them with strings of threadbare and tarnished tinsel and she relished being the object of so many covetous glances.

But her status was not to last. There was a sudden murmur of jealous wonder when Boglina made her entrance and Hagnakker stomped away, hissing in jaundiced rage.

Boglina was undoubtedly the most attractive of the

female rats, which wasn't saying much. What made her the hated rival of every ratwife, however, was not her curvy figure nor her large brown, thickly lashed eyes nor the way she swished her tail as she waddled by distracted mates, but the fact that she had somehow remained single. She was far too independent and pleased with herself for their liking. Why couldn't she be saddled with a good-for-nothing villain like the rest of them? And why did all those stupid idlers find her so fascinating?

That evening Boglina had surpassed herself. Her long black hair had been rolled into mad corkscrew spirals and adorned with the lustrous wings of a dragonfly. Nobody could compete with that and she swanned around, revelling in both the clumsy compliments and the venomous glances she received.

Klakkweena had been too thrilled all day about Fleabee to bother doing anything special, but at the last minute she had knotted some rags in her bristle wig in a haphazard and half-hearted fashion, then scrawled some charcoal squiggles on her furry face and over her ears. She had not told Rancid Alf anything about Fleabee's dream, or the knife. She didn't trust him to keep it a secret and so her peculiar mood had kept him guessing since the morning.

After her earlier exploits, Scabmona had exhausted herself by noon but thanks to several hours' restorative sleep, had prepared herself for the night with the gravity of a general preparing for war.

With a noose around its neck, the throttledoll was slung over her shoulder and Leering Macky's peeler was tucked under her arm. The pinnacle of her hair spike was embellished with the long shiny black legs of Growler, which she had saved for this very purpose. Every time she jerked her head they waggled and kicked furiously. She also wore the frightening blue and silver mask she had taken from the cellar and every ratling wished they had one just like it.

Fleabee watched the gathering crowd with a growing sense of doom. Whatever Mabb had planned for her, it had better happen soon. Even the food couldn't spark her interest and she wondered why Madame Akkikuyu had not made her customary appearance.

Her claws tightened around a ragged bundle in which the ceremonial dagger was hidden, and she told herself to trust in the goddess of the Raith Sidhe.

When Morgan entered, followed by Wormy Ned, he strode to the far corner of the platform and waited for the babble to die down.

'So here we are!' he proclaimed. 'Another Firstblood is upon us, one of the great highlights of our year. Let this be the best blow-out we've ever had. Stuff your ugly snouts till yer belly splits, quaff the grog till you fall down blind and throw yerselves into the hunt later on.'

There was a rousing cheer but he waved it aside and continued. 'Let us not forget whose eyes are on us at all times. Let us be mindful of that and behave as He'd expect, as true rats of Deptford, the meanest, the cruellest, the most vile, infamous scum ever to flush down a gutter. So here's to Him what rules us all – The Great Lord Jupiter!'

During the yells and whoops that followed, the Cornish rat grabbed a bowl of grog from a ratwife who had brought it over to him and drained it in one great gulp.

'Now,' he cried, wiping his dripping jaws on his arm. 'Lemme at that scoff.'

Whilst Morgan applied himself to the nauseating food and the others stared in salivating silence as every fistful was shovelled in, Scabmona decided it was time to begin playing some of her favourite games.

She had prepared several versions of 'What's in the Sack?'. This game was very simple. Something repulsive or alarming was put in a sack which was offered round for others to reach into and guess what that something was. Scabmona had made three separate sacks. One contained the smelliest sludge she could find; another had a tangle of sharp wire and rusty nails, and the third held hundreds of stinging ants.

Presenting these mysteries to the other youngsters was a delight and many squawks of dismay accompanied Morgan's guzzling.

When he had quite finished, the Cornish rat clutched his belly and belched very loudly.

That was the signal everyone had been waiting for. Shrieking with greed, they fell upon the feast in a riotous frenzy.

Fleabee hung back. She was too nervous to eat. There were only four hours till midnight.

Eventually the monstrous supper was devoured and grunts of satisfaction were voiced throughout the tunnel. A decrepit old fogy sang a familiar song of misery and several other old-timers joined in. Scabmona instigated a new game that she had just invented called 'Pinch and Punch' but she was the only one who enjoyed that and no one wanted to take part in her next idea which she called 'Shove off!' while glancing purposefully at the edge of the platform.

Woozy with the grog, some of the ratwives dragged their reluctant mates to their feet to take part in rowdy bouts of kick dancing, tail stomping and hair tearing. Normally Klakkweena would have hauled Rancid Alf into the fray but she stayed close to Fleabee and held her claw when no one was looking.

Appearing more onion-shaped than ever, Rancid Alf staggered over to them. A little worse for drink, he was swaying from side to side, while his tail searched for objects to wrap around and hold him steady.

'Why don't you ask me to go stomping with you?' he asked with a bleary stare. 'What's up with you tonight anyways? You're as jittery as if you'd got wasps in yer wig.'

'I doesn't feel like it,' she answered.

Alf shrugged, then looked at his daughter. 'And how'ssh you?' he slurred. 'Not long now. Not long.'

'I know,' Fleabee said.

Her father surveyed her thoughtfully. 'Be weird without you,' he said at length. 'Never un ... unnerstood you but we got used to your loony ways, didn't we Ma?'

'Leave us be, Alf,' Klakkweena scolded him. 'Your cronies are playing dice over there. Go and join them, and lose your hide.'

'No,' the rat replied. 'I want to play me a game. They're going to be having a bout of 'Tick' in a bit, with real ticks! I doesn't want to miss that.'

And with a lurch, he lumbered off.

The time trotted by until, finally, it was two hours to midnight.

A large metal pie dish had been hung from great hooks in the ceiling and, at a nod from Morgan, it was hammered upon by a rat with a peeler strapped to his wrist in place of a claw.

The noise was deafening and everyone ceased what they were doing.

'It's time, Fleabee,' Klakkweena whispered. 'Mabb will watch over you.'

Morgan held up his arms and all eyes were turned to him.

'Bring out the ratlings!' he yelled. 'Bring out those clean little vermin who are still innocent of the blood!'

The youngsters who had been present at the oath-taking stepped forward. Most of them were keen and ready for the ordeal ahead. Weapons were gripped in their fists and the bloodlust began to gleam in their eyes once more. The tail of a goldfish was still sticking from Lickit's mouth as he whipped out his steel skewer and attacked the empty air with it. A buzz of fierce anticipation crackled through the crowd. What a night this would be.

Only Fleabee was subdued. Her palms were sweating and Klakkweena had to propel her forward to join the others.

Morgan strode in front of them, his sly eyes glinting.

'You all know what you're s'posed to do,' he snarled. 'And what's at stake if you baulk at it.'

They nodded and eyed their neighbours with deadly glances.

'When I bang this 'ere dish,' Morgan continued, 'you leg it out of here into the main tunnels. Then you got just two hours. Two hours to prove yerselves worthy of being a rat. If you don't kill summat by midnight then you'll hear this dish booming away again and know that the chase is on! All our best lads, me included, and anyone else who fancies a go will come tearin' after you and if we catch you, yer done for!'

He bared his yellow fangs in a repulsive, gloating grin and rubbed his claws together.

'Does I make meself clear?'

The ratlings nodded briskly.

'But first of all,' he cackled, 'I done thought up a way of makin' tonight a bit more interestin' fer everyone. Haul it out, Jakey boy!'

A one-eyed rat who had been lurking at the back of the mob came pushing through the crowd. He was carrying a large bulky sack, which wriggled and shook most intriguingly.

Morgan scrutinised the way the others winked and smiled at Jake and his expression turned as sour as Vinegar Pete's. One-Eyed Jake was getting far too popular. Something would have to be arranged to put an end to that, and him.

When he reached him, Jake threw his burden to the ground and a shrill yelp issued from it.

The assembly glared at it eagerly, fascinated to know what was inside.

Morgan dragged it closer. 'This is the best game of 'What's in the Sack?' that's ever been played!' he cried. 'I sent Jakey and the boys out this afternoon on a mission. Now let's see what they fetched back.'

Taking out his knife, he plunged it into the sacking and ripped it open. There was another yelp and Morgan gave the open sack a tremendous tug.

A flurry of arms, legs and a bushy tail came tumbling out and sprawled at the feet of the young ratlings.

It was a young grey squirrel. He was terrified.

A great shout of glee echoed in the tunnel and the squirrel's eyes bulged. His ears flattened against his skull. Lying on his belly, too afraid to get up, he looked searchingly into the murderous faces of his captors and huge tears rolled down his cheeks.

In one movement, Morgan stooped and snatched the animal up by his fluffy tail. The squirrel howled in pain and the rats of Deptford laughed all the louder.

The Cornish rat brought his hatchet-face close to that of the upside-down prisoner and taunted him.

'Long time since one of your lot came on a visit down 'ere,' he said. 'So good of you to drop by tonight.'

'L … Let me go!' the prisoner pleaded. 'Let me go, let me go – for mercy's sake let me go!'

Morgan's eyes narrowed. 'Oh I'll let you go all right,' he promised. 'But you'll wish I hadn't.'

Before the squirrel could ponder on that, Jupiter's lieutenant shouted to the crowd. 'This 'ere has been specially caught fer tonight's fun! The special purpose of this soppy tree-lover is to be a victim fer the ratlings. If they fail by midnight then it and them are up fer grabs. What do you think of that?'

Yammering cheers and whistles erupted.

'Spare me!' the squirrel yowled.

'Oh I can't do that,' Morgan chuckled, relishing the torment. 'You ain't getting out of these sewers alive. That I swears!'

'My Mistress, the Starwife, she … she'll send an army to find me.'

Morgan threw back his head and let loose a great guffaw. 'That mad old hag?' he laughed. 'And a few dozen more gibbering dandies like you? What they gonna do against us, then? Fling their nuts? We'd better scarper, lads!'

Gales of cruel laughter ensued. Then Morgan called for quiet and in a low mocking voice said, 'But we ain't the heartless lags you take us fer. We'll give you a sporting five minutes' head start before these eager young ratlings come bouncin' after yer. How's that for fairness?'

'You're insane!' the squirrel wept. 'Mad, vicious fiends.'

'Aw …' Morgan tutted. 'You just whittled it down to three minutes.'

Snickering brutally, he strode across the platform to where it met the ledge and, with a powerful swing of his arm, flung the squirrel down the tunnel.

The animal bowled helplessly along, then rolled to a slumping halt in a pitiful heap.

'Don't just lie there like a wet bag o' mince,' Morgan roared. 'Shift yerself! Run, run fer your life – what's left of it!'

The squirrel staggered to his feet. He took one final, horrified look at the hundreds of rats whose eyes were shining with a deadly light, and fled.

'There now,' Morgan declared to the ratlings. 'Whoever brings that victim down gets to keep the tail.'

Hurrying over to the metal dish, he took up a stick and prepared to pound upon it.

'It hasn't been three minutes,' Wormy Ned told him.

Morgan chuckled. 'Oh dear,' he laughed. 'What a nasty piece of lying scum I am, after all.'

With that he beat the dish and its thundering crashes reverberated throughout the tunnels, from Bermondsey to Lewisham.

'GO!' he yelled.

Screaming at the top of their voices, the ratlings went charging along the ledge after the squirrel.

Fleabee was the last to leave. Glancing back at her mother for encouragement, she followed the others with leaden feet. Why hadn't Mabb done something by now?

Morgan watched them race away.

'Two hours,' he hissed through his teeth. 'Then I comes to get you.'

12
Terror in the Dark

Whooping and yammering, the ratlings coursed through the passageways brandishing their knives, clubs, skewers and spears.

It wasn't long, though, before they regretted having eaten so much at the feast. They were soon huffing and puffing with stitches in their sides, and feeling queasy. The squirrel had pelted as fast as his legs could carry him and had already disappeared into the dark maze of tunnels.

Uncertain as to which way he had gone, the group quickly split up and Fleabee suddenly found herself wandering alone in the gloomy passages.

With no one around to observe her, she pulled the ceremonial knife from its wrappings and held it in her claws.

'What do you want me to do?' she asked, staring at the dagger as if it could answer her. 'I don't have much time left.'

All she heard were the echoing sounds of feet slapping over bricks in the distance, as the other ratlings spread their searches wide.

Fleabee continued on her way, not caring which course she took. Into the gloomy tunnels she pattered, but the further she went, the more uneasy she became. It grew eerily quiet. The only sounds were those of the flowing water below and her own thumping heart. She had not heard anything of the others for some time. If the squirrel had been captured she would have heard the screams. Perhaps it had escaped? If that were the case, then the ratlings would turn on each other.

At every corner and in every deep shadow she expected there to be a sinister shape waiting to pounce on her. She gripped the dagger more tightly. She would not be able to defend herself with it but the mere sight of its curved blade might put off an assailant.

Minutes ticked by.

'Has an hour gone yet?' she murmured to herself in a thin and fretful whisper.

How much longer till midnight? How much longer till Morgan and his barbaric crew would come charging after them all?

With these dreadful thoughts eating away at her, she

pressed ever further into the sewers, into regions that were unfamiliar and even more menacing.

Fleabee felt vulnerable and afraid. The ghost of 'Orace Baldmony was right – Mabb had lied to her. She had been abandoned.

Even as she reached that wretched conclusion, she looked down at the dagger in her fist, and stopped dead.

A violet light was shining through her claws and, when she uncurled them, she saw that the amethyst set into the bone handle was glowing.

'Mabb's magic,' the ratgirl breathed. 'Whatever she wants me to do, it's going to happen soon. She's going to save me.'

With her eyes fixed on the ceremonial knife, she resumed her journey. After every step, the glimmering light became steadily brighter and Fleabee realised that it was guiding her to where she needed to go.

At the junction of four tunnels she hesitated, unsure of which one to take. Holding the dagger at arm's length, she approached each opening. In the first two the light waned immediately, only to flare and pulse again when she pointed it down the left-hand way.

Quickly she hurried inside. This was an older part of the sewers. The tunnel was narrow and low, and pale mosses grew thickly down the walls.

Blazing like a purple star, the amethyst threw its weird light all around and Fleabee's shadow flew madly about her as she hastened to meet the fate that Mabb had decreed.

Then, without warning, the brilliant light dimmed and darkness sprang back in place about her.

Fleabee gave the knife a shake. She did not understand. The tunnel was long and she had passed no other openings.

Peering over the ledge she wondered if there was something down there, just above the water. She could not see anything.

Puzzled, Fleabee retraced her steps. At once the jewel burst into magical splendour again.

Frowning, she went back the way she had come and suddenly the light disappeared once more.

Fleabee paced up and down the ledge. The light rose and fell. For several minutes she could only stare at the knife and bite her lower lip, unable to solve this riddle. Then she looked up at the wall at her side and reached out with her claws.

The moss grew thickly here. Great swathes of it hung down like curtains. The amethyst flashed and dazzled in her fist. She had guessed correctly.

Pulling the moss aside, she saw that a narrow passage lay behind. The path beyond dropped steeply and Fleabee gingerly ventured inside.

Down she went, the glare from the weapon illuminating the way and Fleabee saw that the walls were covered in drawings. They were crude depictions of battles, scenes of torture and bloody victories. Some of the pictures were so horrific that she could not bring herself to look at them and she turned her head away, only to be confronted by something equally as bad and sometimes worse, on another part of the wall.

The sloping path ended abruptly and she found herself standing before an archway that had been roughly hewn from stones far older than any of those in the main part of the sewers.

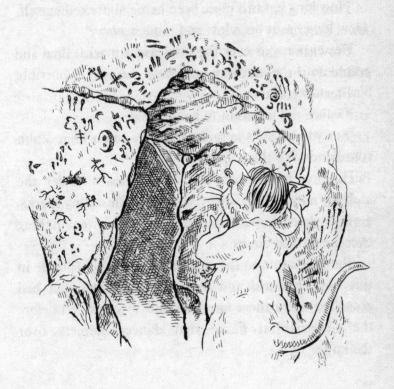

'What is this place?' she muttered, holding the knife aloft so she could get a clearer view.

The rough wall before her had the appearance of immense age. Strange marks and signs had been scratched and gouged into its surface but they were ugly and the ratgirl felt repelled by them. Was it a language long forgotten? What did it say? Was it a warning to keep away the uninvited, or maybe a spell of protection? It looked so ancient that Fleabee doubted if even Wormy Ned would have been able to decipher its meaning.

'How long has this place been here?' she asked herself. 'How long has it been lost and hidden away?'

Her eyes roved over the unpleasant marks, then she peered into the archway but could see only a horrible blackness within.

Fleabee did not want to go in there.

'But you must,' she said. 'You have to do what Mabb commands. It's the only way.'

Holding her breath, the ratgirl passed under the archway and in that instant, with a crackle of tiny sparks, a violet flame leaped from the jewel and went licking over the curved blade.

She had come to the very heart of Mabb's power in this waking world and the musty darkness that had crouched down there for thousands of years fled before the supernatural flame that danced fiercely over the knife.

Fleabee gazed about her. She was standing in a circular chamber with a high domed ceiling. Three stone altars dominated the far curving wall and above them were images of three figures: the headless Bauchan, the Lord Hobb and in the centre – Mabb.

It was a pagan temple dedicated to the Raith Sidhe.

'What am I to do here?' she asked the picture of the Goddess. 'What is it you want of me?'

No answer came, but the unnatural fire suddenly streamed upwards and, to Fleabee's astonishment and dismay, she heard a choking sob behind the altar.

The ratgirl jumped back in alarm. She was not alone – something was in there with her!

'Who is that?' she demanded in a fearful voice. 'Come out! I know you're there!'

There was a second, strangled sob but the sound was filled with such pain and terror that Fleabee forgot all about her own fright.

Stepping forward to the central altar, she peeped over the side.

'Don't kill me!' shrieked a panicky voice. 'I beg you! Please spare me!'

In that same instant, the dagger erupted with a blistering column of livid flame that blasted against the domed ceiling and filled the temple with a lurid, ghastly light.

Fleabee was so taken aback that she almost dropped

the weapon. There, wringing his paws piteously and weeping desolate tears, was the young grey squirrel.

'I ... I didn't mean any harm!' he stuttered through his sobs and snivels. 'I didn't know what this place was. I just wanted to hide. I ... I was running and then ... then I just fell through the moss. Please – don't kill me! Please!'

Fleabee stared at him aghast. Then, with a dreadful sick feeling in the pit of her stomach, her gaze left his petrified face and rested upon the altar. Since the beginnings of time the Raith Sidhe had been worshipped in this temple and dreadful, barbaric rites had been performed in their honour. The ancient stone was blackened and stained with the blood of countless sacrifices.

Her fist that held the dagger

began to tremble. The column of purple flame shook and their shadows shivered as, in that one hideous moment, she finally knew what Mabb intended her to do.

The squirrel's eyes were round and filled with horror. He saw this strange ratgirl turn her attention to the altar and guessed what was running through her mind.

Unable to stop himself squealing, he covered his face with his paws and yowled in despair.

Fleabee looked at the stricken, cringing creature. He was so utterly possessed by terror that his fur was drenched in cold sweat and he was merely waiting for the final blow to deliver him from his unbearable agony.

Slowly, she lifted her face to the painting of Mabb on the wall. The image of the goddess shimmered in the intense light and she could almost hear that coaxing, throaty voice whisper in her ear.

Just one swift action, one sure plunge of the enchanted blade and her promise would be kept and the pact fulfilled. The Raith Sidhe would protect her, Jupiter would be overthrown and she would be High Priestess. The rats of the sewers and beyond would obey her commands and great power would be granted to her. A glorious life was hers for the taking. Creatures from many lands would bow down before her, and all this in exchange for one, insignificant life. The life of a miserable, cringing stranger, who was nothing to her. Why should she care if he lived or died? Better for him to serve a greater purpose, to let his lifeblood summon the sleep visitor into the world.

Fleabee gazed into the golden eyes of Mabb and her own gentle brown eyes blinked away a single tear. The choice was not so difficult for her to make after all.

'No,' she said simply. 'I won't.'

The squirrel wailed even louder, thinking that this was some trick, and he fell on his face, smacking the ground with his paws.

'I won't do it Mabb!' Fleabee called defiantly. 'I can't. I wouldn't kill for Jupiter and I won't for you.'

The image of the Goddess grew dark. The flame that lapped over the dagger was failing.

'Get up!' Fleabee urged the squirrel. 'Get up. We have to get out of here.'

'Don't torment me!' he cried.

'I'm not going to hurt you. I promise. My name's Fleabee, what's yours?'

The sobs subsided and the squirrel reared his head.

'Ambrose,' he sniffed. 'You're not going to kill me?'

Fleabee smiled at him. 'Not even a tiny bit,' she said.

'I don't understand. Why ... what are you going to do? Are you going to wait for the rest of your desperate gang? Is that it? You're going to save me for them, aren't you? I'm going to be ripped apart by the whole savage mob!'

The flame was sinking swiftly and darkness was flowing in from the corners.

'Be quiet,' she told him. 'I meant what I said. I'm not going to harm you. I'm going to help you.'

The squirrel gawped at her. He could not believe his ears. 'You, are going to save me?' he cried.

'If you'll just shut up and let me. Yes!'

'I'm sorry!' he said in a fluster. 'It's just that when I'm scared or nervous I talk too much. I know it's an annoying habit but I can't help myself. My best friend Fitz is always … oh, I'm doing it again aren't I? Thank you for not butchering me, thank you so much!'

Fleabee laughed in spite of herself. 'We're not safe yet,' she said. 'We have to try and escape the sewers, we're both dead if we don't.'

'But why are you saving me? You're a rat of Deptford and we all know what that means. I've heard all the stories. They used to keep me awake at night when I was very little. Oh dear, I don't think I'll ever get a proper night's sleep again after this. Oh, breathe deeply Ambrose, you're gabbling again.'

He took several calming breaths of air, then in a slightly calmer tone of voice said, 'Why would you do this? Why risk your life for mine?'

'Because I don't belong here any more,' Fleabee

answered, running to the archway. 'We'll either get out of this together or die trying. Now, are you just going to stand there yapping, or are you coming with me?'

Ambrose closed his mouth and scampered after her. Together they ran up the steep passage that led back to the sewers.

By the time they tore the hanging moss aside, the flames licking the ceremonial dagger had perished and the light within the amethyst was gone.

'Now she really has abandoned me,' Fleabee said grimly. But there was no time to dwell on that or fret about the consequences. They had to find a way out and Fleabee knew of only two. Both were perilously near the rat domain.

'We have to go back along here,' she told her timid companion. 'I don't know these tunnels. To get my bearings, we need to return the way we came.'

The squirrel's face fell and he was immediately suspicious. 'Back?' he spluttered. 'Back to where all those fiends are waiting?'

'I'm afraid so,' she said. 'But they won't be waiting much longer. Any time now they're going to come swarming after us.'

Ambrose wrung his tail in his paws. 'I'm very afraid,' he said, pressing his lips together to stop himself from launching into a mindless chatter.

'So am I,' Fleabee replied. 'But there's no other way.'

Still clutching the dagger, she began hurrying down the old tunnel, back towards the territories she knew, and the squirrel scurried anxiously after.

During their journey, neither of them spoke, for fear of their voices attracting unwanted attention. Waves of mounting hostility were drifting through the passageways and whenever they heard the slightest noise they whirled around and feared the worst.

Yet they made excellent progress and encountered nothing more alarming than a black beetle.

'I know these tunnels,' Fleabee eventually whispered. 'There's a way out my mother showed me, close by.'

Ambrose seized her arm. 'You mean we really do have a chance to escape this nightmare?' he prattled excitedly. 'Oh thank you. My Mistress will reward you handsomely. If you need any help or advice, then The Starwife is the wisest—'

A horrendous scream echoed down the tunnel.

'We're not out of this yet,' Fleabee muttered, as the scream came to an abrupt end.

'What was that?' Ambrose gulped.

'The other ratlings couldn't find you,' she told him with a shudder of understanding. 'So now they're fighting among themselves. Sounds like someone just lost their first and last battle.'

The squirrel pulled a revolted expression. 'This is a

wholly evil place,' he whimpered. 'Your kind is hideous beyond measure.'

Fleabee could say nothing and they resumed the journey with a heightened sense of the danger they were in. The sound of desperate contests became more frequent. Voices raised in anger were filling the brooding darkness: fierce war cries mingled with dismal yells and blood-curdling screeches ended in guttural gasps.

'It can't be happening,' Ambrose babbled to himself. 'It's too gruesome and grisly to be real. This doesn't happen to a Greenwich sentry – oh no. I'm not used to this sort of thing. Not at all.'

'Sshh …!' Fleabee hushed him. 'Over that pipe, in through that opening and along that wall, there's a metal railing we have to climb and then we'll be safe in your upper world. Can you manage that?'

'I can climb,' the squirrel assured her hastily. 'I'm one of the best – oh by the Starglass, yes I can climb. Like a rat up a … oh, no offence – well, you know what I mean.'

With their goal finally within reach they clambered over a fallen pipe then hurried into the nearby tunnel. A short distance in, they found the rusted railing that led up to the deserted alleyway, close to the scrap yard.

Ambrose stared upward. High above he could see a patch of sky and the moonlight was streaming through.

'I never thought I'd ever leave this foul hole,' he said

tearfully. 'I thought I was going to die down here, die in the most awful, dastardly manner imaginable. I never dared hope to see the blessed sky again.'

He took Fleabee's claw in his clammy paws and shook it vigorously. 'How can I repay you?' he asked. 'Whatever you …'

His voice rasped to a squeak and died in his throat.

Someone was approaching. In the adjoining tunnel, extremely close to them, a ferocious voice was bawling threats.

'Thtop right there!' it yelled. 'I'm gonna twitht thith thpike in your gutth.'

Fleabee recognised the lisping voice at once.

'Lickit!' she breathed.

Ambrose was already halfway up the railing, his tail a whirling blur.

Fleabee was about to follow him when she heard a second rat screaming. Lickit had not been shouting at them.

'Come on, saggy bottom!' the shrill voice shrieked. 'We got unfinished biz, you an' me. You wanna see what little ratgirls are made of? You just try and I'll carve you up like the rude-shaped parsnip you are!'

Fleabee let go of the railing. Her blood ran cold and she turned around slowly.

'Scabmona,' she gasped. 'What's she doing here?'

'Almotht midnight,' Lickit said. 'I couldn't find that

223

thquirrel, nor no one elth neither. I'd have thpiked yer thithter but that one dithappeared ath well. You'll do fine tho'. Therve you right for thticking your thnout where it don't belong.'

'I ain't scared of the likes of you, ya big podgey blah blah!' she countered. 'All talk, you is. You got no chance against me – I'm Scabmona, the saucy savage slaughterer. You can't even say that without sprayin' everywhere. Want me to trim that tongue back a bit for you?'

Lickit gave an infuriated shriek and Fleabee knew he had thrown himself forward to attack.

She ran impulsively to the corner of the tunnel but before she reached it, she heard Scabmona's triumphant whoop. Her sister had managed to avoid Lickit's steel spike.

On the ledge in the main sewer, the two ratlings were squaring up to one another again.

Scabmona was still wearing her mask and Leering Macky's peeler was clutched tightly in one fist.

'Come on drooler!' she taunted. 'That the best you can do? You're rubbish, you are. I bet even Winjeela could take you down.'

Lickit snarled at her. 'I don't care who I kilth tonight,' he snapped. 'I ain't gonna be got by the mob when they come runnin'. You're an eathy enough morthel of prey. Jutht right.'

He lunged at her but she ducked and sprang back. Her peeler flashed out and a bright scarlet line appeared along his side.

'One nil!' she sang gleefully. 'You ain't lisping any more, you ain't lisping any more.'

But the wound served only to inflame Lickit's fury and he leaped at her in a vicious rage.

Scabmona's fearless laughter turned to squeals and she was hard-pressed to avoid his spike. It glittered before her, slicing and slashing.

The tunnels rang with the clamour of their fight.

Scabmona did her best but she was out-matched. Lickit was too big for her and the knowledge that midnight was nearly upon them made his violent attacks all the more desperate.

The ratling tried to fend him off. The peeler hacked and parried, but Lickit drove her back. His arm snaked out, the spike ripped through her mask and tore it from her face.

Scabmona was losing.

With one final yodelling cry, he pushed her against the wall and rammed her fist against the bricks. There was a clang and the peeler fell from her claws.

Lickit glared at her and lifted his spike.

'Your blood will thee me thafe home,' he cackled.

Scabmona glared straight back at him. 'Your breath stinks!' she said with a bold toss of her head that set Growler's legs jiggling in her hair. 'Hurry up and doofer me so I doesn't have to whiff that honk no more.'

'There'th many who'll thank me fer thith,' he hissed, and he drew the weapon back to deliver a fatal blow.

'Maybe they would,' Fleabee said sternly in his ear. 'But not tonight.'

Lickit yelped in a confusion of surprise and fright. The ceremonial dagger was pressed at his throat and he dropped the spike immediately.

'Oh you dozy pudding!' Scabmona groaned at her sister. 'What did you have to turn up fer? I almost had him then, I did. I was all set to give him my speciality, the Scabmona slap! He'd have been on the floor with that.'

Fleabee ignored her and pulled Lickit away.

'Get gone,' she told him. 'Go and find someone your own size to bloomer this night.'

Lickit's tongue flicked the air in dismay. He had been so close. The red gleam of bloodlust blazed in his eyes. He was not beaten yet.

Before Fleabee knew what he was doing, he slithered out of her reach with more agility than she could have anticipated, spun around and smacked her wrist with all his strength.

The knife of Mabb went flying from her grasp. Through the gloom it glittered, scything through the shadows. The amethyst sparkled as the blade went spinning down into the sewer water and, with a splash, it was lost.

Then Lickit pushed her in the ribs and Fleabee was thrown off balance.

On to the ledge she tumbled and, snatching up his spike, he jumped on top of her.

'Thomeone my own thize?' he cried. 'Like you?'

Fleabee was winded and she struggled for breath. Lickit raised the spike over his head to finish her off but he had forgotten about Scabmona.

Like a small, screeching devil she flew at him, biting his nose and pulling on his ears.

Lickit yowled and grappled with her.

Scabmona kicked and scratched and clawed but

eventually he managed to drag her off and, with an angry swipe of his fist, hit her.

The ratling yelped, fell back and hit her head on the wall.

Fleabee watched her sister slump to the ground and the light that suddenly burst into flame in her own eyes did not stem from Jupiter.

From the depths of her being she let loose a defiant, hate-fuelled scream and threw Lickit off.

The ratboy toppled sideways with a horrified wail, then Fleabee was grabbing him by the throat and hitting him with her clenched claws.

Holding him by his hair, she pulled him down and knelt heavily on his chest.

Lickit could not move. His head was jutting out over the ledge and the sound of the rushing water filled his smarting ears.

The bloodlust dimmed in his eyes but Fleabee's own deadly gleam was still burning fiercely.

Scabmona rubbed her aching head and was astonished to see what was happening.

Fleabee had taken up Leering Macky's peeler and was holding it in a steady, iron grip before Lickit's frightened face.

'Go on!' Scabmona cheered. 'Doofer him! We can go back to Old Klakk and Rancid Alf with his tongue waggling on a stick, like a captured enemy flag.'

Her sister tensed and pushed the peeling blade against Lickit's exposed throat.

'Do it!' Scabmona urged.

Fleabee bared her teeth and Lickit squeezed his eyes tightly shut.

'No, Child.' A gentle voice broke into her anger. 'Do you really want to remain here?'

Fleabee raised her eyes and, sitting on the ledge on the opposite side of the tunnel, was the ghost of 'Orace Baldmony.

A faint glimmer of green light shone about him and he was shaking his head benignly.

''Ere!' Scabmona cried. 'Who's that?'

'Put the peeler down,' 'Orace told Fleabee.

'He hurt my sister,' she answered hotly. 'He … he's like the rest of them down here, brutal and cruel. No one would care. Don't you see? What's the point of it all? Nothing changes. They're all murdering scum! Who cares?'

'I do,' the ghost said. 'If you murder him then you really will be a true rat of Deptford at last, and there'll never be any hope of escape for you.'

'Oi!' Scabmona yelled. 'Shut up Granddad. I wanna see him bloomered.'

Fleabee stared at 'Orace's kindly face, then looked down at Lickit once more. He was just as terrified as Ambrose had been in the temple and the rage died in her soul.

'Get up,' she told him.

'What you doing?' Scabmona squeaked in outrage. 'Don't let him get away, you lardy lump!'

Fleabee stood aside and allowed Lickit to stagger to his feet. The ratboy backed away and shamefully stared at the ground.

A frantic booming gong suddenly reverberated through the sewers and the dark air shook all around them.

It was midnight.

'The other rats will be hunting now,' 'Orace said. 'Morgan and his crew will be on the prowl. Any youngsters who are not drenched in the blood of their first kill will be preyed upon.'

'That means you, Dribbler!' Scabmona chuckled at Lickit.

'I have to thcram,' Lickit cried in panic. 'I have to ethcape.'

Turning tail, he fled down the tunnel before anyone could stop him.

'Not that way!' Fleabee called. 'They'll catch you!'

But he took no notice and ran headlong into the darkness.

'Now is the time for us all to depart,' 'Orace said. 'Well done, Child. The upper world awaits you.'

Fleabee thanked him and the ghost's eyes glittered back at her. There was a breath of wind and he dissolved into the air like early mist burning away in the sunshine.

'Who were that?' Scabmona demanded, greatly impressed. 'You never cracked on you had a spook friend.'

Fleabee smiled. 'That was 'Orace Baldmony,' she replied.

Scabmona spat automatically then kicked herself. 'You should've said,' she grumbled. 'I'd have asked him how much it hurt when his head were pulled off. Now I'll never know.'

A shy, nervous cough broke her macabre train of thought.

Ambrose the squirrel had courageously climbed back down the railing to see what had happened to Fleabee.

'Are … are you remaining here?' he asked. 'Only I can't stay any longer. I can't believe I came back to find you. I'm not naturally this heroic, in fact I think I must be deranged. Why haven't I darted outside? I could be halfway to Greenwich by now. Fitz won't believe it when I tell him. I'm gabbling again, aren't I?'

Scabmona scowled at him then tugged on Fleabee's elbow.

'What's he on about?' she cried. 'You ain't goin' nowhere are you?'

Fleabee looked into her sister's belligerent face.

'I have to,' she told her. 'If I don't go then Morgan

and the others will be coming for me as well. You're all right – you're too young to even be out here on a Firstblood. I have to go.'

'What, and never come back?'

'Never.'

Scabmona stuck out her chin and tried to make herself look aggressive.

'Can't believe you're running off with the dinner,' she hissed, jerking her head in the direction of Ambrose. 'Shocking waste that is, specially its fancy tail.'

Fleabee gave her a sad smile.

'Goodbye,' she said.

Scabmona cleared her throat and blinked. 'What'll I tell Old Klakk and Swelly Belly?' she asked.

'Just tell Mother I'm going to continue making her proud for as long as I'm able – she'll understand that.'

Her sister shook her head in disgust. 'Barmy you are,' she said.

'And you'll be the most feared ratwife in the whole of Deptford one day,' Fleabee said.

'Scrap that! I want Morgan's job.'

To Scabmona's revulsion her sister leaned forward and hugged her tightly.

'Get off!' the ratling snapped, hastily disentangling herself and surreptitiously wiping her eyes.

In the distance, there came a baying uproar and

Scabmona sniggered wickedly.

'Reckon they've found Lickit,' she declared, reclaiming the peeler. 'He's finally gone and got hisself well and truly licked – haw haw.'

She took a deep breath and a mischievous twinkle danced in her eyes.

''Ere, have this,' she said pushing the throttledoll into Fleabee's arms. 'I don't need it no more. I've outgrown it. 'Sides, you won't forget me so quick having that.'

Before Fleabee could protest, Scabmona turned and went charging down the tunnel.

'If I'm quick I might get me some souvenirs!' she called back. 'They might even pull his head off and we can have a kickabout!'

Fleabee waited till her sister's squat little figure disappeared in the remote gloom. Then she followed Ambrose back to the railing.

The moonlight was pouring from above and when Fleabee stepped into its silver light, her tears shone like milky diamonds.

'I'll take you to Greenwich,' the squirrel told her, as he began the climb. 'The Starwife will aid you.'

Fleabee took one last look at the dark dank sewers that had been her home for so long and remembered everything that had happened to her in them. She thought of the way the sunlight transformed the squalid holes to glittering gold and how she had loved watching that hidden beauty creep out of the darkness. Then she thought of her family and knew she would not see any of them again.

'Quickly,' Ambrose urged. 'We must go to Greenwich at once!'

Fleabee shook her head.

'No,' she said. 'I'll go my own way. I've listened to others for too long. It's up to me now, I'll decide what to make of the new life that awaits.'

'But what will you do? How will you survive? There are dangers up there you know nothing about. I've seen and heard such terrible things!'

A determined smile appeared on Fleabee's face. 'Who knows?' she said. 'Maybe I'll become a ratwitch like Madame Akkikuyu. It's in my stars, after all. Or maybe I could learn how to breathe fire and perform with gerbils and a hamster. It really doesn't matter. The entire world is mine to roam in.'

Kissing the throttledoll, she slung it over her shoulder and started the climb to freedom.

Up she went and soon she was breathing the cold clean air of her new life.

'I'll never go back to the sewers again,' she swore. 'Never! I'm on my own now and ... I'm the happiest I've ever been.'

Fleabee's Fortune

The wheel of destiny is always turning. The ancient powers that once ruled the world in the first darkness are indeed waking and nothing can prevent their return. Unstoppable forces are already in motion.

The time of the old Gods is dawning.

In that forgotten temple, deep underground, other sacrifices will be made, and the Raith Sidhe shall walk amongst the living once more.

Ferocious battles will be waged in the name of the Lord Hobb and the King of Night himself will return to torment the unhappy world. A new age of despair shall befall us.

And in that terrible time Mabb, the sleep visitor, will remember the ratgirl who cheated her. Mortals cannot thwart the Gods and escape their wrath forever. No matter where Fleabee's fortune leads her, one day after many years have passed, she will eventually be drawn back to Deptford – down to the very sewers she vowed she would never enter again.

When the Three Thrones are rebuilt and suffering fills the land, Fleabee and Mabb will confront each other one final time and in that fateful moment, the doom of all things will be decided ...